HEART'S APPRAISAL

By the Author

Broken Fences

Promises to Protect

Heart's Appraisal

Visit us at www.boldstrokesbooks.com

HEART'S APPRAISAL

by

Jo Hemmingwood

2025

HEART'S APPRAISAL

ISBN 13: 978-1-63679-856-1

THIS TRADE PAPERBACK ORIGINAL IS PUBLISHED BY
BOLD STROKES BOOKS, INC.
P.O. BOX 249
VALLEY FALLS, NY 12185

FIRST EDITION: AUGUST 2025

CREDITS
EDITOR: ANISSA MCINTYRE
PRODUCTION DESIGN: STACIA SEAMAN
COVER DESIGN BY TAMMY SEIDICK

Acknowledgments

I must thank my wife, Chelsey, who is my first sounding board, and my editor, Anissa, who helps me hone my story. Thanks to Rad, Cindy, Sandy, and the rest of the crew at BSB who make the magic actually happen. Finally, thank you to the village that raised me and taught me what it means to live in community.

For Chelsey, my muse.

CHAPTER ONE

The first time Andy drove to the little community outside of Huntsville, she'd gotten hopelessly lost in the backwoods and farmland. Getting lost had surprised her. Andy was accustomed to driving in the metropolitan and downtown areas of Birmingham and had reasoned that country driving couldn't be more difficult than that. She had been wrong. There were roads that seemingly went to nowhere, roads that ended at pastures, roads that weren't roads. And very few of the roads had signs.

She was proud she had found Green Valley much more easily this second go-around. She guided her Mercedes coupe gently over a set of railroad tracks. The pastures and fields rolled past like a vast, green sea. Here and there cows dotted the horizon, but mostly it was corn. So much corn.

Andy slowed and looked for her turn. It would be on the left past a small, one-lane bridge over a muddy creek. It was easy to miss because of a big tree that nearly blocked the road from view.

Something caught her attention on her right. It was the figure of a woman with an apron around her waist. She had a straw hat on her head and a crude bag thrown over her shoulder. She was clipping the weedy, white flowers by the side of the road and stuffing them into her bag.

Andy took another look at the flowers. They were spindly with disc-shaped clusters of flowers on top. They looked like the same weeds that had been growing for miles along the roadways, but this woman was carefully collecting them. *Hmm.*

The turn Andy had been searching for suddenly appeared. "Shit!" She hit the brakes, but it was too late. Mumbling and glowering at the voluptuous figure of the strange woman behind her, Andy was forced to drive past and look for a suitable place to turn her car around.

When she came back to the turn, the woman had moved a bit further down the shoulder of the road but looked up with a tilt of her head. Andy couldn't make out her face beneath the broad brim of her hat, but she could feel the woman's eyes watching her. Andy kept her own gaze determinedly forward and swung onto the hidden road.

It was potholed and rough. *The road couldn't have been this rough back in February.* It turned to dirt and gravel in another half a mile, but Andy couldn't remember if that was before or after the road's fork.

She slowed for a flock of chickens unhurriedly crossing the road and smiled. The birds were lucky the asphalt was so rough. There was no way to speed, and so the fowl were relatively safe. She pulled forward cautiously lest one of the hens impulsively decide to dive back beneath her car. She continued down the remote, bumpy road.

She took a right at the fork and, another quarter of a mile on, hit the red mixture of gravel and clay. Dust kicked up behind her, but she looked ahead for the big magnolia trees that flanked the drive of her late great-aunt's house. Aunt

Darcy had passed nearly six months before and had left no children. Her substantial property had been passed to Andy through her father, the son of Darcy's younger brother.

After the very high-profile and disastrous Arnold trial of which Andy had been a part, she'd been eager to get out of Birmingham for a while. Her knuckles whitened on the steering wheel as a steaming wave of shame passed over her remembering Benjamin Arnold's greasy smile. With a deep breath, Andy forced her thoughts from the courtroom and the firm and onto the task at hand.

It had taken three months to get her realty license. She'd spent another four months learning the ropes from a wizened old man named Calvin Harvey. He'd been mostly deaf but was a good family friend and knew the business backward and forward. She'd got her feet wet in Birmingham but had decided to relocate to Green Valley.

Huntsville was growing in leaps and bounds, and its borders were constantly stretching. On her first foray to Green Valley, Andy had noticed all the land and, more importantly, all the *For Sale* signs. There was money to be made out here for a certainty. Andy liked to think she had an eye for good opportunities. That was what success in realty was all about, according to Harvey. She looked forward to setting her own pace away from the rat race of criminal law. Climbing the corporate ladder no longer appealed to her. From now on, she was her own boss.

Lost as she was in her thoughts, her great-aunt's house was suddenly upon her, magnolias looming like dark-foliaged sentinels. Andy slowed and took the left turn, crawling slowly up the hill to the two-story, gothic revival home.

It was clear that in the years of Aunt Darcy's decline, the house and gardens had gotten away from her. Andy made a note to hire a good yard person in addition to a carpenter. She didn't think a whole crew would be necessary to return the house to good form. It had been built in the 1920s but had been updated thirty years before to include central heat and air, and a few other staples of modernity.

She parked her coupe in the rear of the home beneath the carriage house awning and unfolded from the car. With a stretch to the peeling paint of the carriage house's ceiling and then to the cracked concrete beneath her Italian leather loafers, Andy marveled at the stiffness that had accumulated in her muscles. *It was a two-hour drive, after all.*

She retrieved her travel bag from the passenger seat. The car door made a smart, snapping sound as Andy shut it. She gingerly ascended the derelict stairs of the back porch. They seemed sturdy enough for her weight, but they probably needed to be replaced. Andy sighed. With another mental addition to the mounting list of to-dos, Andy unlocked the back door and let herself into her new residence.

❖

Hazel had watched the sweet little coupe approach out of the corner of her eye with interest. She hadn't recognized the vehicle. When it had missed its turn, presumably because the driver had been staring at *her*, Hazel had bitten down a grin. The Mercedes had proceeded down the road to the old Jackson store, turned around and come back. She'd been busily gathering the yarrow but had spared a glance long enough to notice it was a blonde driving.

She tipped back her straw hat and wiped her sweating forehead with the back of her hand. Her bag was full, though she did gaze greedily at the lazily swaying heads of the yarrow blooms stretched before her. Shaking away the impulse to gather more, she cinched her sack and turned to trek back to her green Subaru. Darcy's voice echoed in her head. *Only ever take what you need.*

It was not the first time she had heard her departed friend speak to her. Darcy had passed six months ago at the age of eighty-five, and Hazel missed her fiercely. The elderly woman had been like a grandmother to her, and Hazel felt her loss in a very primitive, physical way. It was Darcy that had taught her how to use herb craft to ease her father's Parkinson's symptoms.

Hazel had heard that Darcy's property had gone to a distant relative, and the small community had waited for weeks to see what would become of it. Nothing had happened. No one had claimed the estate, and so they had all relaxed.

Her wandering thoughts snapped back into focus as she tossed her flowers in the back seat of the 1975 4x4 Wagon. She remembered the little coupe and was a bit uneasy. Darcy had lived on the same road the stranger had turned down, right across from Hazel and her father. Surely no one she knew drove a Mercedes C-class. No one in Green Valley, anyway. Most folks in her town drove pickups or SUVs to accommodate the terrain.

Once she pulled her car across the highway and onto her little country road, Hazel speculated more about the blonde behind the wheel. She really hadn't gotten a good look. If the woman had pulled into Darcy's drive, though, her father would notice. He noticed every going and coming of every vehicle that drove past their home. His small, glass greenhouse was conveniently placed to allow him to monitor traffic. And if *he* didn't notice, his service dog surely would. Nothing got past Nubi. Hazel smiled. She fiddled with the sweaty hair sticking to her neck and tried to put the worry from her mind as the sun sank lower on the horizon and cast the road in stripes of shadows.

❖

Andy had just finished moving the last box of stuff to the edge of the yard in front of the house. She swiped at a trickle of sweat that rolled down the side of her face and then cringed at the dust on her hands. She had entered the house the day before and found boxes upon boxes of clothes and knick-knacks stacked on the handsome cherrywood table in the formal dining room.

She hadn't known her great-aunt that well and didn't consider herself a sentimental person. The idea of going through everything was exhausting, and so she had opted instead to simply set the boxes out and allow them to be picked up as trash.

The only things she had saved from the purge were a couple of pairs of old denim, a soft, purple button-down overshirt, and a pair of ancient lace-up boots. After all, if she was going to be working at the house, she would need clothes to work in. All the clothing fit surprisingly well, though it was somewhat strange wearing a dead woman's wardrobe.

The ensemble made her feel like an imposter. Glad no one from Birmingham could see her, she turned back to the house and trudged the soft grass of the yard to the porch. She pushed the door open and traipsed through the spacious foyer and other rooms to the back of the house where she entered the kitchen on the right. There, she took down a blue rose-patterned mug and poured herself a steaming cup of coffee from her press.

Andy leaned on the well-worn wooden butcher block that

served as an island and tapped her fingernails on the surface. The clicking sound echoed around the room, reverberating off the glass-front cabinets and making the house seem incredibly empty. *Not empty...lonely. The house seems* lonely. There was a hollowness to the home as though it was accustomed to bustling, energetic activity. She wondered briefly if houses could mourn. A small, rueful chuckle escaped her lips. *Ridiculous.* With a shake of her head, Andy pushed the melancholy aside. Certainly, this house was no lonelier than the once well-decorated downtown apartment she'd emptied and left behind.

The memory of her polished, modern furniture and the stainless-steel kitchen she'd rarely used surged to the surface of her mind. *Everything black and white and so very, very clean.* It was nothing like this house with its patterned curtains and thick area rugs covering the highly trafficked hardwood floors. But then again, she was looking for a change.

This move had been the perfect opportunity to reinvent herself. With that opportunity had come the question about what it was that Andy truly wanted. She had never spent much time contemplating what she desired for herself. She'd gone to law school because her father was an attorney, and once in the world of barristers, Andy had wanted what the partners at the law firm had wanted. She'd bought a Mercedes and joined a country club and taken up golf. She bought expensive wine and hosted exclusive, catered parties at her apartment. There was absolutely nothing wrong with any of those things, but she'd never stopped to wonder if those were really *her* things.

Andy turned abruptly at a knock at the front door, splashing coffee across her hand.

"Damn!" She wiped her hand on her jeans before striding through the butler's pantry, the formal dining room, and out into the foyer once more. She could make out a warped figure through the diamond-patterned glass panes in the front door and opened it without a clue of what to expect.

There was a curvy brunette on the porch who looked vaguely familiar. The woman smiled and offered her hand.

"Good morning, I'm Hazel Quinn. My father and I live just across the road."

Andy grasped Hazel's hand and quickly took in her slightly Roman nose and olive skin. Her chestnut hair was pulled half-back, but the rest of it fell in waves down her spine. It was her eyes, however, that were her most striking feature. They were an amber color, like a bird of prey. She wasn't classically beautiful, but there was something incredibly compelling about her. Andy smiled back, flirtatiously flicking one eyebrow.

"Good morning, Ms. Quinn. I'm Andy Richter. The late Darcy Richter was my great-aunt."

"Yes...You look like her."

"Really?" Andy was taken aback. She cast her memory to the little time spent with her aunt and tried to find the resemblance.

Hazel nodded. "Something about the set of your mouth and jaw looks exactly like Darcy." Hazel smiled at her again. "I noticed that you put quite a lot of boxes out on the road-side."

"Yes. I just didn't have the fortitude to go through it all." A thought struck her. "Was there something you were looking for?"

"No, the only things I wanted were her photo albums, and I got those. Which brings me, actually, to the reason that I came over." Hazel rummaged in the bag on her shoulder for a moment and then produced a key.

The way she dug around in the bag... "You were on the roadside yesterday. Picking flowers."

"Oh, yes. The yarrow helps with some of the side effects of my father's medication."

"A flower does?" Andy edged back slightly. Hazel was pretty, but Andy had known a lot of pretty women who also happened to be batshit crazy.

Hazel smiled as though she'd read her mind.

"Yes, a flower." She offered the key again. "This is a spare key to the back door that Darcy gave me years ago. I thought the appropriate thing to do would be to give it to you."

Andy took it in hand and looked at it thoughtfully.

"Was my aunt in the habit of giving out keys to random people?" She noticed the color rise in Hazel's face.

"I'm hardly a *random* person. I knew your aunt nearly all my life. We were good friends."

"I should probably have the locks changed." Andy spoke more to herself than to Hazel.

"These are good people around here. No one would just walk in."

"So, you're saying there are more of these keys floating around out there?" Andy studied Hazel's face as her amber eyes flashed.

"The local hardware store would have what you need," Hazel said in a distinctly cold voice. "Don't forget to put a padlock on the root cellar." She turned and stepped off the porch. Andy watched her go. She had a light, flowing gait Andy found incredibly sexy.

"Padlock on the root cellar," she mumbled and then also stepped off the porch to circle the house. She didn't remember there being a root cellar and felt a bit foolish at the thought of Hazel pulling one over on her. However, on the southeast corner of the foundation a pair of doors led under the brickwork that surrounded the house. A rusty latch held the doors closed, but it moved smoothly with the first tug.

Andy drew back the doors apprehensively and turned on her phone's flashlight before stepping down the brick stairs and onto a packed earthen floor. She swept the light around to find shelves stacked with jars of what looked like canned goods. Stepping further into the cellar, she noticed something swinging overhead and found bundles of dried herbs and braids of garlic.

"More stuff?" Andy sighed and circled the shelves as she wondered if her great-aunt had been some sort of doomsday prepper.

She took down a jar to find snapped green beans with a neatly labeled lid. The date was a year before, and Andy realized she knew nothing about canning or the shelf life of such goods. She would have to throw it all away.

With the threat of botulism hanging in the air, Andy put the jar back and turned to go. She wouldn't bother to put a padlock on the cellar door. If anyone had plans to steal any of Aunt Darcy's canned goods, they were welcome to them.

❖

By the time Hazel walked back across the road to her home, her father had drunk his coffee and was puttering around in his greenhouse. She let herself in and watched him gently touch each plant with his large, calloused hands as he checked them for insects and rot.

"How did it go?" he asked softly without turning to her. She sat down heavily on an overturned five-gallon bucket.

"It could have been better." Nubi, her father's service dog, came to scoop his nose under her hand. She absently stroked his black fur.

"Oh?" He did turn to look at her this time over the top of

his plain, wire-rimmed glasses. He looked every bit the retired history teacher he was. "How so?"

Hazel leaned forward, pressing her elbows into her knees. "I don't know, Pops. She's not like Darcy at all." Hazel realized that had been her hope. She sighed. Her dear friend had been so warm and gentle, but this Andy woman was neither of those things.

"What *is* she like?"

She thought back over the conversation. "Wary."

Her father harrumphed in what Hazel suspected was humor.

"Of course she is. She doesn't know us or this community. It's our job to welcome her. Leviticus says, 'When a foreigner resides among you in your land, do not mistreat them.' We are supposed to love them like family."

"You're right, Pops." Hazel sighed again. She did not generally subscribe to organized religion and specifically had beef with much of how Leviticus was applied, but at least Moses got the bit about strangers right. "But you didn't see her face. She just *knew* she was better than me."

"You're saying she's haughty? Is that the…what's the word?" He squinted at her for a second. "Is that the *vibe* you got?"

Hazel smiled. "Yeah, that's the vibe I got. And you know I'm rarely wrong about these things."

He nodded solemnly. "Your intuition is usually spot-on, Wildflower. All I'm saying is to give her a chance. Make her feel welcome."

"Of course." She rose from the bucket and stretched her spine like a cat. "Just don't hold your breath on being friendly with her."

"I always take it one day at a time."

Hazel smiled as her father turned and recommenced the tender ministrations to his seedlings and flowers.

"I know, Pops. I know." She meandered back to the house and let herself in the front door, kicking off her sandals by the chest in the foyer. Barefoot, she padded to the kitchen and began tidying to try to keep her mind from how irritated she was with Andy Richter.

Disdain. The word floated to mind. That was it. There was something in Andy's manner that had been incredibly dismissive. She hated to admit how disappointed she was that Andy's resemblance to Darcy was only skin deep. Hazel had been hoping for a friendship. For someone who might help her keep Darcy's memory alive. She'd clearly been wrong about that.

Hazel rinsed the coffee pot and rummaged in the freezer for dinner ingredients. Her father typically had friends over for a game of poker on Saturdays, and she made something like nachos or spaghetti that would feed a large quantity of people. Little did they know she used low-sodium recipes and ground turkey meat. It was the least she could do for their cholesterol.

She didn't mind the noise or the mess of company. It kept her father in good spirits, which was, in her opinion, just as important as the actual medical treatment he was receiving for the Parkinson's. That was another gap Darcy left when she passed. She would often bustle in on a weekday with a bouquet of fresh flowers, a question about a potted plant, and something home baked. She would sit with Paddy Quinn for a couple of hours and then breeze away, leaving a glittering aura in her wake.

Hazel smiled as a wistful feeling filled her chest. The sensation faded abruptly when she thought again of her new neighbor. The only aura Andy Richter seemed to have was cold and frosty. Even her eyes were like ice; a sharp, penetrating, light blue that brought to mind a frozen lake. Her blond hair, cut angularly along her strong jawline, was silvering at the temples, adding to the Ice Queen image. Hazel had noticed the silver in her hair with surprise and wondered if Andy was graying prematurely. By what Hazel could judge, Andy seemed to be around her own age, mid-thirties. Stress could cause that sort of color change, but it was hard to imagine the aloof, mocking Andy Richter being that affected by anything. She cut such a stolid figure. Andy was a bit taller than Hazel and enticingly square across the shoulders. Though it could have simply been Andy's stiff posture that gave this impression.

After a moment Hazel realized she had been staring at the wall across the room as she traced her mouth idly. She shook herself from her reverie. Andy was gorgeous, she could admit that much, but Hazel was *definitely not* interested in a woman who thought herself superior. And Andy clearly did.

"No, thank you," she said aloud. She pulled the spread of washed yarrow that had been drying on the island toward her. Bundling and prepping herbs would cool her temper and take her mind off her cold neighbor. She hoped.

CHAPTER TWO

Tuesday afternoon, Andy visited the local hardware store. It was a small building with an appliance rental warehouse attached to the rear. She stepped from her coupe, hyperaware of the discord between her attire and her Mercedes, and pushed open the door. A jingly tone announced her arrival, and a few men looked up from where they were convened around the checkout counter with a newspaper.

She could smell coffee burning and the oily, metallic scent of machine parts. The men, deciding she didn't need their help, went back to the newspaper over which they were arguing. Andy scanned the labels hanging above the tiny, merchandise-crowded aisles. She took several decisive steps forward and was immediately overwhelmed.

Andy was the first to admit she wasn't terribly handy. She could count on one hand the number of times she'd actually been in a hardware store. It had always been simpler to hire someone for the rare repair or replacement, and so it had seldom been necessary for her to navigate the world of nuts and bolts and tools. However, she was determined to do this one thing on her own before the actual renovations commenced. It just seemed like starting off on the right foot.

When she finally found her way to the appropriate aisle and section, she was disappointed at the selection. She took a few things from the shelf and flipped them back and forth. It had crossed her mind to simply order what she needed online, but she hated the delay of returning and reordering if something wasn't just right. As she frowned at the nearly indecipherable instructions, a voice called to her.

"Can I help you, ma'am?"

She looked up to find a man she judged to be in his late fifties addressing her.

"Maybe." She smiled without showing her teeth. "I need to change the locks at my house."

"Well, let's just see what we've got here." He ambled down the aisle, taking a pair of reading glasses from his shirt pocket as he approached. He held out a hand, palm up. Andy handed him the knob and lock sets she had been contemplating.

"This house is very old, and I was looking for something more in the antique department."

The man met her gaze, and Andy was startled to see a pair of bright, amber eyes. "Are you the one who's moved into Darcy's place?"

"I am. I'm her great-niece, Andy. And you must be related to Hazel Quinn."

The man grinned. "I'm Amos. Hazel is *my* niece. Made her acquaintance, then?"

His smile was so genuine Andy couldn't help smiling back. "I have, yes."

"Good. Not many young folks in this town anymore. Now about this." He refocused on the knobs. "We don't have anything old-timey like what you're looking for, but if I might make a suggestion?"

"Sure." She nodded.

"So long as the equipment is in good condition and it's just new locks you're wanting, consider just putting in a key-lock deadbolt at every door." He reached past her and grabbed an installation set for the deadbolts. "Preserves the original handles and knobs this way."

Andy took the deadbolt set in hand and smiled. "Thank you, Mr. Quinn."

"Don't mention it." He walked back to the counter. Andy grabbed a couple more sets and then followed him to the register. "And if you need any help, give Paddy or Hazel a holler. They both grew up in this store."

"Did they?" She laid the three sets of deadbolts on the counter.

"Oh yeah. The shop is called Green Valley Hardware now, but it used to be Quinn's Hardware. Our grandfather opened the shop back in the fifties."

"A family affair, then?"

"A mess, more like it." He laughed and gestured to the card reader with the total. "There are a lot of places around town that used to have the Quinn name on them." Andy didn't miss the note of pride in his voice. "Hazel keeps up with all that now. *She's* the entrepreneur. The rest of us just march in time."

"I see." Andy took the bag of hardware and smiled. "Thank you again for your help."

"No problem." He came around the counter to hold the door for her. "And when you get ready to hire a contractor for the old place, give me a call. I know a few guys that do good work."

"Of course." She smiled again. If she still lived in Birmingham, Andy would call around and ask for quotes from various contractors, but she accepted that things worked differently out in the country. It was likely that Amos Quinn *would* know the best person for the job. Perhaps she would give him a call when it was time.

❖

Hazel got home around five to discover her dad had grilled hamburgers. She stepped through the back door and her mouth watered. Nubi greeted her with a happy nudge, and she affectionately rubbed behind his fuzzy shepherd ears.

"Something smells great!"

"Nothing fancy." Paddy laid her plate at her seat and handed her a cold beer. "Just burgers and tater wedges."

"Well thanks, Pops."

"You're welcome, Wildflower. I know Tuesday is bank day and it can be a bit hectic." He sat across from her with his own burger. "And I have a favor to ask."

Hazel groaned in appreciation as she bit into the burger. Pops always got the seasoning just right on his burgers. She realized what he had said and swallowed hard to answer him. "Sure, name it."

"I think our new neighbor needs some help."

She was instantly cautious. "Andy. Why do you think that?" She continued to nibble on her burger.

"She was cursing a blue streak on her front porch this afternoon. I think it was something to do with locks."

"You didn't walk over?"

He looked at her shrewdly. "She seemed to be having a bad day. I didn't want to come across like I was mansplaining."

Hazel covered her mouth and laughed. "Mansplaining can only happen if you're explaining something to a woman that she already knows. You couldn't mansplain doorknobs to Andy Richter."

He shrugged. "All the same. It might come better from you."

She hesitated. Hazel wanted no part in trying to aid Andy after the cold rejection she'd received a few days ago. But it was the right thing to do. Hazel nodded. "Alright, but I can enjoy this burger first, right?"

"Of course! That's what I made it for."

Half an hour later, Hazel walked past the big magnolia trees toward the Richter property. She mounted the porch and knocked on the door. After a moment, Andy slowly opened it. She had a tumbler of something dark and alcoholic in her hand. Andy blinked as though surprised.

"Hey there, I know this is weird, but my dad is under the impression you could use some help?" Hazel felt increasingly stupid as Andy just stared at her. "With your doors or something?" she added lamely.

"Oh, I—uh…" Andy seemed to stiffen. She was *definitely* deliciously broad across the chest. "Yes, actually, I believe I could use some help."

"Really?" Hazel felt like an ass when Andy frowned. "I mean *great*. How can I assist?"

"Come in, Hazel." Andy said suddenly and motioned her into the foyer. "The bugs are getting in."

"Oh, right." She followed Andy to the back of the house and into the kitchen. It looked incredibly empty in comparison to the way she remembered it. There were still a couple of old aprons hanging by a nail near the back door. Hazel went to them immediately and fingered the soft, scalloped neckline of the faded blue one. She turned to find Andy watching her and felt heat rise to her face.

"I'm sorry."

"Don't be. Take them." Andy brought the glass to her mouth. "I don't cook." She took down another tumbler and gestured to a bottle of scotch. Hazel nodded. "Or install deadbolts, apparently."

"Deadbolts." Hazel took the offered glass and sipped. It was incredibly warm and smooth. *I could get used to this.*

She pulled herself back to the task at hand. "You were trying to install deadbolts?"

"Yes. Your uncle at the hardware store suggested deadbolts instead of replacing the whole handle and lock on each door. It was a great idea, except that I have never been much of a handyman." She topped off her own glass of scotch and then continued. "You would think someone with an education would be able to figure it out based on a YouTube tutorial. My only consolation came when I realized I didn't have the right tools for such a repair."

"So, you don't own a drill or a hole saw?"

Andy shook her head slightly. "No. I've never needed power tools."

Hazel was not surprised in the least. She tried to maintain a neutral tone though a small part of her wanted to gloat. "Well, I'm pretty handy, as it happens, and I *do* own a drill and hole saw."

The frosty gaze slid over her face. "Oh?"

Hazel took another sip of the expensive liquor to extend the moment. "I can come over in the morning, if you would like, and sort it for you."

For all her calm reserve, Andy answered very quickly. "That would be much appreciated. I can pay whatever fee…"

Hazel laughed and waved a hand, causing Andy to trail off. "There's no fee for neighbors, Andy."

"Well, then…" Andy seemed at a loss. "If there is ever anything I can help you with, you will let me know."

It wasn't a question. Nor did it feel like a suggestion. It

seemed, to Hazel, like a command, and she wondered exactly who Andy Richter was.

"What sort of things would be in your wheelhouse, if you don't mind me asking?"

"Real estate...and criminal law."

Hazel's eyebrows shot up. She'd never been good at hiding her emotions, much to her frustration and chagrin. "Well, I can't say there's much need for criminal law here, but there is a lot of real estate for sale these days."

"I'd noticed." Andy seemed to study her over the rim of her glass. "Your uncle mentioned that you are an entrepreneur."

Again, not a question. A statement. Hazel couldn't believe she hadn't noticed the courtroom presence before. To be fair, she'd never seen a criminal trial. But looking at Andy now, Hazel could easily picture her completely in command of a courtroom.

The image was more than a little sexy. Hazel pulled her thoughts to the present.

"Uncle Amos likes to say that, but the truth is far less impressive."

"Oh? Do tell." There was a glint in Andy's pale blue eyes that Hazel couldn't quite decipher.

"Well, the Quinn family owns several properties and I'm in charge of keeping track, more or less. I take care of the books. You know, the retail income, worker wages, taxes and such. I also make repairs here and there as needed. It keeps me pretty busy, but it's never dull." She shrugged. Truthfully, it was a *lot* of work, but Hazel had stepped into the family business at a young age and found herself more than capable. She enjoyed the organized chaos of it.

"How many properties?"

"Green Valley Hardware and Appliance, Valley Grocery,

Quinn's Pharmacy, and the Corner Stop and Shop." She ticked the businesses off on her fingers. "And we own a few vacant storefronts along Main Street. There's actually a negotiation going on now to put in a little café within the year."

"Quite the business magnate, aren't you?"

Hazel laughed at Andy's dry tone. "Sure, I'm just raking in the green." She met Andy's gaze. "What about you?"

"What about me?" Her smile lingered, but Hazel detected a shift in the room.

"Why swap from criminal law in the city to real estate in bumfuck nowhere?"

Andy's face went blank, but not before Hazel glimpsed something that looked like regret in her eyes. "Burnout." After a brief hesitation, Andy continued. "I got tired of dealing with criminals. Now, what time can I expect you tomorrow?"

Hazel didn't skip a beat at the abrupt change of subject and tone. There was definitely something there worth digging into if she cared to do so, but she wasn't sure she did care just yet.

"Will eight o'clock work for you?"

"Eight is perfect," Andy said with a nod.

Hazel finished her scotch and put the glass on the counter. "Thanks for the drink."

"Of course." Andy gestured behind her to the aprons. "Take those."

"Thank you, again." Hazel felt silly repeating herself, but didn't know how better to express her gratitude. She gathered the aprons. "I'll see myself out."

Andy waved vaguely, but her eyes were still sharp and calculating. "Good night, Hazel."

"Good night."

❖

Andy swirled the liquor in her glass as she watched Hazel leave. She glanced at the bottle of scotch and was tempted to top off again but thought better of it. She knew how the bottom of that bottle looked, and she wasn't eager to see it tonight. Taking her half-empty glass with her, she walked across the open hall of the foyer to the study. The spacious parlor off the left of the foyer had a few pieces of heavy furniture and wide bay windows, but Andy preferred the intimate feeling of the study. In the original blueprints the room had been a bedroom, but Darcy had used it—as far as Andy could tell—as an art studio.

Darcy had left numerous sketchbooks and there were a dozen canvases of still life and landscapes propped along the wall, most of them unfinished. Of all the rooms in the house, Andy felt most comfortable in this room. The corner windows faced northeast and afforded a view of an overgrown vegetable patch and several empty bird feeders. She could make out the edge of the woods at the back of the house. The trees stood in a deep, velvet green silence. Andy wondered, not for the first time, how far back they extended.

Turning from the window, she sat in a battered but soft brown leather chair before a low, wooden coffee table. As the table was already scored with deep gouges from God only knew what, she didn't feel bad propping her feet on its scarred surface. Andy allowed herself to sink into the leather and breathe for a moment. The room still held the scent of paint even after months of vacancy. There was something else underneath the paint, something like dried flowers, something Andy couldn't quite place.

She sighed into the empty house and took a sip of scotch. Her thoughts turned to Hazel Quinn, and one side of her mouth rose in a half-smile. Such a surprise she was turning out to be. When Amos Quinn mentioned his niece was an entrepreneur,

Andy was sure he was exaggerating. However, for a small town, Hazel oversaw a good slice of it. She probably ran almost half of the businesses in town.

And she's handy. Andy had a certain type of woman she usually pursued. Capable, driven, and elegant. She liked women who had their own thing going and weren't overinvested in her life. Andy liked relationships that bolstered her image. She wasn't ashamed to admit it. It was easier to manage her life without the complication of deep emotion.

Hazel wasn't what Andy would call elegant, but she was definitely alluring. Her amber eyes were striking and that abundance of chestnut hair just begged for the tangle of her fingers. Andy could imagine running her hands down Hazel's shoulders and spine. She could almost feel the lush curves of Hazel's body beneath her fingertips.

Andy blinked away the image and took another swallow of scotch. It trickled like firelight down her throat. Whatever she might envision doing to Hazel was not actually going to happen. If Hazel was anything, she was complicated. Deeply entrenched in the community, living with her ailing father, and offering her services to any and all neighbors. She painted a clear picture of a woman who could not do simple or shallow. You don't ask a person to change who she fundamentally is, especially a person like Hazel Quinn.

❖

True to her word, Hazel was on Andy's porch the following morning at 7:55 a.m. She was dressed plainly in a T-shirt with cropped jeans and carried a toolbox. Andy had not been awake long but was dressed in her borrowed clothes. Hazel stared momentarily when she opened the door.

"Something amiss?"

Hazel shook her head. "No, you just…" She hesitated but then smiled. "You look just like her sometimes."

"Aunt Darcy? Hmm…" Andy stepped out onto the porch with her coffee cup as Hazel arranged her tools on the small, wrought-iron bistro set beside the door. "I never thought we favored that much."

"Well, you do. It's more than just features, though, it's something in your expression, I think." She turned and looked at Andy. "I've got pictures of her. Candids of when she was younger. I can bring them over sometime if you'd like."

Is this how we become friends? "That would be nice." Andy gestured to the door. "How do we start?"

Hazel grinned. "We pop the pins."

Andy supposed this was some sort of euphemism but quickly found—as Hazel wielded a well-used hammer—that Hazel meant it quite literally. Andy helped Hazel maneuver the door as they removed it and propped it against the porch railing. Hazel then took out a drill and the aptly named hole saw.

Andy was impressed. Hazel was very organized and seemed to know exactly what she was doing. Andy felt little more than useless as she fetched tools and hung about while Hazel installed the bolt on the front door and the back kitchen door. When they reached the side door leading into the study, however, Hazel turned to her with a smile and handed her the hammer.

"What am I to do with this?" She tried to act casual as she hefted the unfamiliar weight in her hand.

"Pop the pins."

Andy looked at her suspiciously. "You're going to make me do this one? Are you sure you want me handling your tools?"

"You're not going to break them, Andy." Hazel grinned.

She had a smear of something grease-like along her jawline that Andy thought suited her.

"That's what you think," she murmured before turning to the door. "I'll give it a try."

It took her much longer to install the bolt than it had Hazel, and Andy wasn't convinced it didn't look a little bit crooked. Standing back and surveying the work felt good, though. She was sweating profusely, and she couldn't remember the last time she had done that outside of a fitness center. Pulling her shirt to wipe her face, she turned to find Hazel watching her.

Hazel dropped her gaze and pivoted to look at the door. "Pretty good work for a lawyer."

Andy smiled. "Thank you for your help today."

"Of course."

They walked back to the front porch, where Hazel began to pack away her tools. Once she finished, Andy watched her wipe her grimy hands on a handkerchief. Hazel then straightened with a smile. *She really is quite pretty.* Lost as Andy was in surveying the curve of Hazel's hips and thighs in her denim, she didn't immediately realize Hazel had asked a question.

"What's that?"

"I was wondering if you had listed any properties yet?"

"Oh, not yet. I was actually going to ask you about the properties you own downtown."

"Oh?" Hazel frowned for the briefest moment. "What about them?"

"Would any of them be suitable office space, I wonder?" Andy leaned casually against the porch railing and crossed her arms over her chest. "I need business, and it just makes sense to have a place to *do* business."

"That *does* make sense." Hazel tapped a finger on her chin

for a moment. "Actually, there is an old storefront downtown on the north side of Main Street. It served as a hair salon for some time, but it's been updated with modern electric, and central air and heat."

"That sounds promising." Andy didn't want to give away her little jolt of excitement. She had driven downtown with an eye out for rental space only to find that much of the old square needed major renovation. She believed she could snatch up portions of it for cheap but would also need to sink major money into updating the buildings. And for that, she needed a few good sales.

"We can set up a time for you to take a look at it, if you would like."

"Sure, I'm pretty free these days." *That isn't a phrase I'd ever imagine saying.* Flashes of her Birmingham life streamed through her mind like the colorful whirl of a carousel.

Hazel smiled. "Really? Not found any hot nightlife here?"

Andy took the teasing with grace but smiled slowly and let her eyes freely rove Hazel's body. "Not yet."

Hazel blushed. A beautiful rosy color glowed on her olive-tanned skin. "How about Saturday?" Hazel asked abruptly and blushed more. "For the rental space, I mean. Saturday morning around nine?"

Andy smiled again. "That works for me."

After Hazel had given her both the directions and the address to the potential office space, Andy let herself back into the house. She collected her tape measure and notebook from the kitchen counter and went into the study. Thanks to a copy of the house's blueprints, she had the dimensions of the rooms. The entire house would need to be painted, and the floors refurbished before she could decorate or refurnish. But the study was her favorite spot, and she was determined to make over at least one room for herself.

She wanted very badly to have an area that felt like *her*. The new her. The *her* she was slowly discovering.

First was to purchase a thick, expensive area rug for the floor and an office desk she'd spotted in an antique shop in a nearby town. It wouldn't be much in the way of décor, but it would be a start. She didn't want to commit too heavily to one style or another. She wanted to give herself room to grow and experiment with what she liked. Then she could carry that style through the rest of the house. But it was important to her to get this room just right.

CHAPTER THREE

"Hey, Pops. What's up?" Hazel answered her phone as she pulled into a parking spot on Main Street.

"I was wondering if you would mind picking up dog food while you're out and about today. It slipped my mind to add it to the grocery list yesterday."

"I guess I can do that, but tell Anubis he's behind on rent."

Paddy laughed. "Oh! And guess who came to visit me just after you left this morning."

Hazel watched a few people coming and going on the sidewalk. "Who?"

"Barney Jackson."

She frowned. "Who?"

"Barney! You know him. We went to school together. His mama was a Parson. They lived over there by Frankie."

It was easier to just pretend she knew to whom her dad was referring. "Oh, yeah. Barney. What's he been up to?"

"He was an accountant in Huntsville. Just retired. Said he came in last weekend for the fishing."

"Well, how about that?" Hazel glanced at the time. "I hope his catch was good."

"Between you and me, Wildflower," he began in a

conspiratorial tone, "Barney never was much of a fisherman. Nor much of a hunter, truth be told."

"Well, it's a good thing he lives in Huntsville." Hazel glanced at the cars driving by. "Hey, Pops, I've got to go. I'll get Nubi's food on the way home."

"Right, right, wasn't trying to keep you. See you later."

"Later, Pops."

Hazel ended the call, exited her car, and then fit the key into the lock of the storefront door. When she entered, she flipped the switch on the overhead lights. They didn't illuminate. *I'll have to call about that if Andy wants to rent.* She noted the need to call the water board as well. The small salon that had previously occupied the space had closed months prior, but there was still a lingering smell of permanent wave solution and hot irons.

It was a long room divided into two spaces. The front area was well lit by large south-facing windows originally used to lure shoppers when the space had been a clothing store. Hazel turned back to prop open the door with a lonely brick. Once the air was stirring, she made her way across the ancient floorboards to the back room, which had been used for customers needing a hot wax. It was decently sized, and Hazel thought it could make a good private office for Andy to consult with clients. There were even a couple of narrow windows positioned near the ceiling for additional light.

She thought she heard the door and so retreated from the room to peek into the front space. No one was there. The brick had slipped, letting the door inch closed half a foot. Hazel scolded the little rush of anticipation.

Foolish. She remembered blushing earlier in the week. Even now, she could feel the ghost of that heat in her face as she recalled the seductive smile on Andy's face and the way her piercing eyes had lowered to leisurely study her body before meeting her gaze again with a smirk.

Hazel wasn't unaccustomed to being given the once-over by women or men, but it was the first time it had stirred something in her that she hadn't been able to put to rest. Just recalling the expression on Andy's face raised her temperature in response. She'd had some relationships with women. She wasn't *out* in her community just because it was never talked about and there had never been a relationship intense enough for her to want to bring it home to her father.

There was something about Andy that made her feel completely out of her depth. She was sexy and sophisticated and naturally intimidating. Not that *she* was intimidated, Hazel reassured herself with force. But there was little doubt in her mind that Andy would be a demanding and experienced lover. Hazel had never been into dominant play, but it was all too easy to imagine with Andy. *If I was interested.*

There was a creaking sound and Hazel turned to find that the door *had* opened this time. Andy stepped through the entrance with a cursory glance around, and Hazel experienced a pleasant shock at seeing Andy in business attire. She wore high-waisted, cream slacks and a pale blue oxford shirt with small cream pinstripes. Her platinum hair just brushed the collar of the shirt and glinted in the sun behind her. She would be perfectly at home in front of judge and jury.

Hazel tried very hard not to stare. She strove to act as though she had supermodel, courtroom Barbies dropping in on her every day.

"Good afternoon!" She stepped from the doorway and shadows of the back room.

"Ah, good afternoon, Hazel." Andy removed her designer sunglasses and leveled those incredibly blue eyes at her.

"Okay finding the place?"

"Sure." Andy turned and glanced out of the windows. "I have to admit it's a prime spot. On the square, no less. Hard to imagine a business going under in this location." She raised her brow.

Hazel took her meaning immediately. "Oh, the salon owner retired." She smiled and hoped it would soothe Andy's suspicious mind. "The shop wasn't mismanaged or anything."

"What a relief."

"Right." Hazel stepped forward, suddenly aware of how inelegant her blouse, prairie skirt, and sandals looked in comparison to Andy's outfit. "So, the front room has a good bit of space, but there's a back room that could work as an office…"

They talked about the building's amenities and shortcomings. Andy wanted to know if there was additional parking in the back and if she could paint the walls. Hazel was willing to let her do pretty much anything but change the exterior face of the building or knock out walls. An occupied building was far better than an empty one as far as she was concerned.

They haggled good-naturedly about the rent and settled on a price that was in the upper range of what Hazel had been hoping. All in all, the meeting had been a success. She passed a copy of the key over to Andy.

"That one opens the back door, too."

"Great." Andy looked down at it and arched a brow. "And you're the only one with the other copy?"

Hazel grinned. "I promise." She walked Andy to the door. "I'll call about the water and electric on Monday and I know a good crew for painting if you need one."

"That sounds great."

"I'll have Gavin stop by Monday around 3:30?"

Andy gave her a cool smile that didn't meet her eyes. "Sure."

Hazel arched a brow. "What?"

"What?"

"You look suspicious again."

Andy seemed to relax and gave Hazel a slightly warmer half-smile. "You are very perceptive."

"I've always been good at reading people. It comes in handy."

"Indeed." Andy seemed to hesitate for a moment as her eyes followed the path of a large dust mote in the sunlight. "I was only wondering why you seem so invested in my success."

"Why shouldn't I be?"

"I—well…" Andy narrowed her eyes. "I don't know."

City people. "Look, I'm sure I don't need to explain microeconomics to you, but the short of it is that this town needs new blood. It needs people to put some money into it. If you can get people buying and selling property here, that would be a success for everyone. So yeah, I'm invested in your success just like I am in the café opening down the street. More business is good for everyone."

"That's a very holistic view. You must be thrilled that Huntsville is growing so quickly. There will be a suburb out here in no time."

Hazel felt her face contort of its own accord. "No. Suburbs are not what I want." She couldn't keep the disgust from her voice.

"Oh? Why not? More business, right?" Andy's brows were raised, and she was looking at her expectantly. That note of disdain had disappeared, however. She seemed genuinely curious.

"Suburbs are noisy, and they can ruin a small town's economy. They're also not great for the environment. Clearing forests and pastures to cover with gravel and foreign grasses that outcompete our native flora? It's a terrible use of space." Andy looked somewhat surprised, and Hazel realized belatedly that her vehemence seemed disproportionate to the issue. "I belong to a local conservation group." She hoped Andy would accept this explanation.

"Was Aunt Darcy in this group?"

It was Hazel's turn to be surprised. "She *was* actually. How did you know?"

"I found an old leaflet in her art things. It was for Green Valley Conservation Club."

"That's us."

"Is that where you learned the thing about the yarrow?"

It took Hazel a moment to realize what Andy was asking. "The yarrow? Oh! No, that was Darcy, too." She paused and then took a gamble. "Which reminds me, actually. I meant to ask you if I could forage in your woods."

Andy's face froze and Hazel realized how the question sounded. She ignored the sensation of heat creeping up her neck and tried to keep her expression open and inquisitive. It had been a sincere question, after all.

Andy cleared her throat. "I don't think there's any yarrow in my yard."

"No, there isn't, but behind the house there are woods and past that a small pasture. There are quite a few useful herbs in both locations."

"Well, in that case, you are free to visit my forest any time." Andy's tone was neutral, but there was a twitch at the corner of her mouth.

"It would just be a few times a season."

"Yes, I imagine you are too busy for regular foraging. You seem to have a finger in every pie around here."

The glimmer of humor wasn't gone from Andy's gaze, but it was now coupled again with suspicion. Hazel recognized her wariness and felt the need to defend herself. "It's good to be involved in your community. The secret to personal success is collective success. Or that's how I was raised."

"Hmm." Andy made a dubious sound that seemed to Hazel like dismissal. She didn't argue, however. "Well, I won't keep you. We both have quite a lot to do, it seems."

Hazel followed Andy to her parked coupe and bid Andy goodbye. She watched as Andy carefully pulled into traffic. Hazel raised her hands to her face. The embarrassed heat was fading as she wondered if Andy was naturally suspicious or if experience had made her that way. Hazel recalled the conversation they'd had over the expensive scotch in Darcy's kitchen. Perhaps she was being too hard on Andy. She couldn't imagine a criminal defense attorney holding on to optimism for very long.

Hazel was an idealist, but she had been telling the truth when she'd said she believed that the community prospered when everyone was successful. Perhaps if Andy stuck around long enough, she would see that too.

❖

Andy wasted no time choosing paint colors and perusing area rugs for the downtown office. The original hardwood planks were too pretty with their alternating whorls and patches of amber and copper to cover entirely. A few nice rugs would add some dimension, though.

She had just stepped back to consider the colors she had quickly, but not carelessly, brushed on the walls when the door creaked open. A slim figure was silhouetted by the afternoon sun slanting in. As the figure came more fully into the room, Andy realized it was a young man. *This must be Gavin.* She turned to meet him.

"Ms. Richter?"

She stepped forward to offer a handshake. His grasp was firm. "It's just Andy."

He grinned. "My mama would whoop me if I called a lady by her first name." His smile was infectious. It stretched his freckled face pleasantly as he ruffled his auburn curls.

"Well, I wouldn't do anything to anger your mama." Andy returned the smile. "You are Gavin?"

"Yes, ma'am, I am." His hazel eyes glanced behind her to the paint-testing wall. "Those the colors you've narrowed down?"

She stepped back to allow him to pass. "Yes, I'm leaning more toward the green. It's professional, but cozy."

"I agree." He nodded seriously. "And it will look great with the old floors in here."

Andy was pleasantly surprised that the teenager had echoed her precise thoughts. She contemplated him more seriously. "You do a lot of painting projects, Gavin?"

"Painting and a few other things."

"What about replacing light fixtures?"

He looked up at the uninspired, circular light fixtures overhead then back at her with a twisted grin. "I've got a buddy who works with electricity."

"A buddy…"

He must have picked up on her skeptical tone because he turned serious once again. "I've got a whole crew, actually. They'll be on my dime, Ms. Richter, and I'll manage them."

"So long as you do." She looked at him with her sternest expression and he gave her a winning smile. Andy had just decided she liked Gavin when the door opened again.

A robust man in his fifties walked in and wiped his boots on the dusty mat at the door. Andy clocked the ostrich leather boots and the turquoise rings he wore before even giving his face a cursory glance. *A potential patron.* She gave him her full attention but feigned a casual air, infinitely thankful she had decided against wearing her great-aunt's well-used boots that morning.

Praying to the universe this guy was not a random individual who had just wandered in, Andy greeted him and gestured toward the office in the back. As he sat down in the secondhand chair, he introduced himself as Ernest Hardy.

"Mr. Hardy, what can I do for you?" Andy settled into her own well-preserved chair and leaned back confidently.

"Well, I saw your sign on the drive in."

"Mmm, I was hoping that was a good investment." She flashed her teeth.

"It sure caught my attention."

Andy noted his drawl and the tan line as he adjusted his Rolex. If Ernest Hardy wasn't exactly local, he wasn't a city-boy either.

"I'm assuming you have some property you're looking to put up for sale."

He nodded. "I do at that. My father passed in December, and I inherited his property and home."

"And you have no interest in holding on to it?"

"I considered it for a while." He rubbed his blue-stubbled chin. "Thought about putting some horses out there, but really it's just too much trouble. I live in the city limits of Huntsville now and would have to hire someone to keep an eye out."

"How much property?" Andy took out a notepad. She didn't really need to take notes—she had an excellent memory—but found people took her more seriously if she looked to be copying their dictation.

"It's one hundred acres plus a farmhouse, a stable, and a barn."

Wow. This was exactly what she had been hoping for. A big parcel of land she could break into smaller tracts and auction. "Farm equipment?"

"I've already handled all that." He tapped his booted toe on the ground and leaned forward. "Honestly, Ms. Richter, I have an idea what the land and house are worth, and I just need help getting what I can out of it."

This was exactly what Andy wanted to hear. She smiled. "Mr. Hardy, I will do my very best."

Hazel was weeding between her lavender bushes when a shadow blocked her evening sun. She shielded her eyes and found Andy standing there, looking deliciously cool in a button-up with the cuffs rolled and a pair of jeans that hugged her lean legs. How she could look that enticing in a simple outfit was beyond Hazel.

"Good evening," Andy said. Despite her aloof demeanor, there was something eager in Andy's eyes that gave Hazel the idea she had news to share.

Hazel removed her gardening gloves and stood with no small amount of protest from her cramped knees. She'd gotten lost in her work, as was common, and she would pay for it with soreness in her shoulders, back, and thighs the following day.

"Good evening," Hazel replied with a smile. "Productive day?"

"I hope so."

Hazel fanned her heated face and swiped at the sweat

creeping down the back of her neck. "Would you like some lemonade?"

Andy arched a brow. "Really? You have lemonade on hand like that?"

The shade of the porch did nothing to help the feverish blush on Hazel's face. "Is that any different from you having fifty-dollar-pour bourbon *on hand*?"

"Hmm. It seems so…" Andy settled into an oil-finished rocking chair and crossed her legs neatly. "Mayberry."

"There's a reason *Andy Griffith* was a popular show," Hazel reminded her. "I'll be right back." She escaped into the cool of her house and went immediately to the cupboard to pull down a couple of glasses.

Andy often seemed to be mocking her. Did Andy truly consider herself superior or was it just a habit to use that tone of voice? Either way, Hazel didn't particularly care for it. So far, she had swallowed any aggressive retorts, but it was becoming increasingly difficult. Her father would have some anecdotal wisdom about keeping her damned mouth shut, but she couldn't conjure up the will to quote the scripture to herself.

The waft of tangy citrus scent that escaped when she poured the lemonade brought Hazel back to herself. She took the perspiring glasses in hand and returned to the porch. And to Andy's smirk. The ice tinkled as she handed Andy a glass and then sat in the second rocking chair. Her feet flexed instinctually, and she slowly rocked in the chair. Back and forth, she moved rhythmically and surveyed the flower beds critically while trying not to care if Andy liked the lemonade.

"Mmm." Andy made a satisfied noise in her throat and then cut her frosty eyes over to Hazel. "This is homemade. No store-bought lemonade could taste like this."

Hazel was a bit too pleased that Andy was pleased. "I did make it from scratch. Rolled all the lemons by hand."

"There's something herbal in it."

"Ah, yes. Mint. I grow it on the south side of the house under the kitchen window."

"Pleasantly unexpected."

"I'm glad you like it." Hazel took a sip of her drink and then placed the glass on the large wooden spool that served as a side table for the porch. "Now, tell me about your productive day."

Andy visibly rolled the lemonade around in her mouth and then set the glass aside. "I've got my first client." She looked across the space between them to smile at Hazel. "Ernest Hardy."

"Hardy?"

"Do you know him?"

"I'm acquainted." Hazel's mind flipped through her personal Rolodex of community and familial information. "I think he's around my dad's age. Grew up in Green Valley. His father just passed away around Christmas."

"You do know everyone."

Hazel shrugged. "When you're as involved in the community as I am, it's hard not to."

"Indeed." Andy raised one brow. "Well, he doesn't want to keep the property so we're going to break it into tracts and—"

"Break it into tracts?" Hazel couldn't help the interruption. The property, she was envisioning was a prime, rural estate.

Andy cocked her head. "Yes, tracts—and auction them off separately."

"Auction them?"

"Is there a reason that's a bad idea?"

Hazel considered her words. "People around here might not be into an auction."

"They will be if they want the real estate."

Hazel bit her tongue hard and managed a noncommittal hum.

But Andy persisted. "What? What is it you are trying not to say?"

The monotonous creaking of the rocking chairs on the aged boards of the porch seemed suddenly loud in the space between them. Hazel watched a butterfly light gently on her lavender and tiptoe to the top where it opened and shut its wings with a slow, regular rhythm. Like a steady breath beating in a smudgy collage of orange, fawn, and cream.

"People in Green Valley are accustomed to land passing from hand to hand either through family or outright purchase. Auctions are for cattle, not for real estate, as far as they are concerned. They prefer things much more straightforward than that." Hazel also longed to say that it felt as though Andy was trying to take advantage of the people in her community, but she didn't have any evidence to support this theory.

"It *is* all straightforward. I don't see how it's different from cattle."

"No, you wouldn't." Hazel sighed. How could she explain to this woman that land, unlike cattle, was considered enduring? It was one of the few types of real, measurable wealth accessible to the citizens of Green Valley. It was something invaluable they were able to pass into posterity, unlike cattle, which were often destined to trade hands several times before their final destination.

For the first time, Andy turned her head and faced Hazel fully. She pinned Hazel with cold eyes. "What do you mean by that?"

Hazel imagined the intense gaze had been utilized in innumerable courtrooms. "I mean that you don't know these people. My community. My people."

"People are people." Andy spoke with such certainty Hazel was almost convinced.

"To a certain extent, yes, but I think you'll find that the priorities of folks here differ from those of the folks in Birmingham."

Andy returned her gaze to the yard before her. Hazel watched the butterfly suddenly take flight, startled by something only it could sense. A slow, soft roll of thunder crested in the distance, a drum wrapped in thick velvet. A gust of wind stirred lazily, bringing the thick smell of rain with it.

"Storms the next couple of weeks." Hazel smiled crookedly. They were now talking about the *weather*. She was uncomfortable with Andy's tactics, but she wasn't going to avoid the real topic at hand. She cleared her throat. "When is the auction?"

"Two weeks."

"At the Hardy farm?"

Andy scanned her face again. "Yes. At ten o'clock on the Monday."

"I'll be there."

"Given this conversation, I didn't take you to be the sort for an auction."

"You don't know me very well."

Andy laughed. It was a soft chuffing like the sound an amused tiger would make. *Even her laugh is sexy.* Really, it wasn't fair.

"I suppose I don't. I should rectify that. We are neighbors, after all."

"We are indeed."

"I wonder how my expensive liquor would taste in your lemonade."

It was so casual and yet delivered with such a suggestive tone that Hazel swallowed hard. "Are you asking me over?"

"If you would be open to that."

Hazel realized the pace of her rocking had accelerated and forced herself to ease off. "Sure. I'd like to see the work you've done on Darcy's home."

"My home, you mean."

Hazel arched a brow. "Does it really feel like yours already?"

Andy smiled, but her eyes remained cool. "Feeling has nothing to do with it." She rose smoothly but abruptly from the chair. "Thank you for the lemonade, Hazel. I have a great deal of work to do between now and the auction." Without waiting for a reply, Andy was down the steps and gliding across the yard toward Darcy's home.

"You're wrong," Hazel murmured. "Feeling has everything to do with it."

"What's that?" her father's voice called from the other end of the porch where he was steadily making his way up the short set of steps.

"Nothing. Just thinking aloud."

Paddy swiveled his head to watch Andy stop at the dirt road, look both ways, and then walk briskly across to the shade of the magnolias. "Hmm." He sat down heavily beside her. "Something to do with our neighbor?"

She sighed and leaned back into the chair, releasing her surprisingly tense muscles. *That's Andy ache, not gardening ache.* "She just doesn't get us. I don't know that she can."

"Of course she doesn't get us." Paddy took off his glasses and polished them meticulously. "She's not from here. As for the latter…" He looked to the gap between the towering trees where Andy had disappeared like an elegant shadow. "That remains to be seen, Wildflower. You can't judge what a person can or *cannot* know."

"True." The butterfly had returned, and Hazel followed

it with her eyes. "But she's so damned certain of herself. It doesn't seem that she has any desire to know us."

At this, Paddy surprised her by chuckling. "Give it time, and she might not have a choice."

CHAPTER FOUR

Andy retrieved her leather briefcase and retreated to her study. When she'd driven by Hazel's house and seen her outside, she had been compelled to walk over. Andy had not stopped to analyze this impulse. She'd simply left her case on the kitchen counter and walked out the front door.

The conversation had been stirring. She loved the spark of confrontation in Hazel's voice. Andy lived for confrontation. It was a part of her nature. The feud of wit and will was an arena in which she thrived, and Andy was pleased, despite her abrupt departure, that Hazel seemed to be well-equipped for sparring. Though Hazel had hit a sore spot with her last comment about Darcy's home.

No. She ate and slept and brushed her teeth here, but it didn't feel like home. She'd become accustomed to the sounds of the wind whistling around the corners and the lazy grazing of the walnut limb on the south wall. Andy knew well the feel of the cold bathroom tile when she forgot her slippers or the way the kitchen sink dripped if you didn't turn the handle at the perfect angle. Despite her familiarity with the house, though, she still felt out of place, and she didn't know how to fix that. Mostly, she tried not to think about it.

Andy placed her briefcase on the study coffee table before pouring a glass of bourbon from the square-sided bottle. She sat in the soft leather chair and then carefully unpacked the case to arrange information about the Hardy Estate into stacks. Andy contemplated the assortment of data and maps before her but couldn't get her brain to dial in. Hazel's earnest, golden eyes kept flashing to mind.

"Damn." She stood, lowball glass in hand, and paced to the corner of windows to glare into the gloaming. The sun setting at the front of the house hit the tree line at the back of the house with a vibrating, orange glow. It gave the flakey bark of the pines a soft, fuzzy appearance, and Andy had the unprecedented impulse to caress the trunks with her fingertips.

She's getting to me. She took a sip of liquor and savored the smoky burn of it. Andy could still hear the creak of the rocking chairs and taste the lemonade's tang on her tongue. Hazel was the most *real* person she'd ever met. She was genuine and earnest in a way that spoke of a woman who truly knew herself. *And she has a way of cutting me deep.*

It was this that had prompted Andy to leave so abruptly. She who had never run from anything, who thrived on confrontation, had run from Hazel's probing. *Feeling has nothing to do with it.* She couldn't believe she'd said that. Andy sighed and turned from the window. Such a callous thing to say and *not* what she actually believed.

Andy was an expert at mastering her emotions. In the courtroom, this had been essential. Focusing on the facts of a case and presenting them in a way that benefited her client was her specialty. More than once, she'd uttered that exact line in the courtroom. *Feeling has nothing to do with it.* But she was no longer in a courtroom. And using facts and logic to keep people at a distance just wasn't as important as it once had been. She had been shocked at the emotions Hazel's query brought to the surface. And maybe a little ashamed.

Hazel was *really* getting to her. How could she even begin to explain herself to someone like Hazel? Someone who ate, slept, and breathed her community. Someone who drew people to her rather than pushed them away. Someone woven into the fabric of her surroundings the way a tree would grow around an object in its path. As much as Andy enjoyed Hazel's company, she feared they were too manifestly different to—

To what? What was it she wanted to avoid or instigate? A friendship? She was pretty sure a friendship was safe territory, even with so many differences. But...it wasn't friendship that Andy could picture with Hazel. It was something deeper. Deeper than anything she'd wanted before.

And now she had come to the real reason she had left Hazel on the porch so hastily. More than feeling vulnerable and exposed, Hazel had demonstrated to Andy what it was to feel *seen.*

Even if Hazel had laid Andy bare, she was oddly comforted that such a thing was possible. Hazel had instinctively, or by some other uncanny ability, known that Andy had not settled into the house.

The house still felt like Darcy lived here. Which wouldn't have bothered Andy except that she had never really known her great-aunt. So far, she'd convinced herself that the house was a project and the little self-expression she'd allowed herself in this room was just to designate it as headquarters for her schemes and stratagems.

Adjusting to the pace of life in Green Valley was a hurdle. Andy was much less further along in setting up her business than she had planned. In Birmingham, anything was possible, and on any timetable. Here, people closed on Sundays and had reasonable business hours that ended at seven p.m. This was simultaneously refreshing and frustrating. It was a quaint selling point for the properties Andy hoped to get her hands on, but it set her timeline back quite a bit. She had hoped by this point she would already have a few properties.

As it was, the Hardy family property excited her with its possibilities. Despite Hazel's doubts about her methods, Andy was confident she knew what she was doing. With new vigor, she set her mind to the task of working out the tracts of land and setting a base market price. It was tedious work, but Andy was not daunted and rushed to put into writing the work she'd already begun in her head. This was just what she needed to launch her brand in Green Valley.

❖

Hazel shielded her eyes from the sun as she approached the massive white tent that had been pitched in front of the late Joe Hardy's well-kept farmhouse. Andy had outdone herself. The setup wouldn't have been out of place in Huntsville or Birmingham. As it was, it did seem out of place in Green Valley.

"Quite the circus." Paddy's mouth twitched as he cut his eyes to his daughter.

"And there's the ringleader." Hazel had spotted Andy. She looked stunning in a sleeveless off-white blouse and green trousers. Designer sunglasses hid her eyes, but Hazel thought she detected a shift in Andy's stance and a subtle smile on her lips as Hazel, Paddy, and Anubis made their way forward.

"Hazel." Andy smiled and then held out her hand. "And you must be Patrick."

"Paddy." He corrected Andy with a grin.

"And Nubi." Hazel pointed to the black shepherd mutt.

"Newbie?"

It was Hazel's turn to smile at the skeptical expression on Andy's face. "Nubi. Like Scooby with an *n*. It's short for Anubis."

"Ah." Andy's expression cleared. "That is much more fitting." She looked at Nubi's lolling tongue and dripping saliva. "I can tell he's a very good boy." At the words *good boy*, Nubi tilted his head, and Andy let out one of her small chuckles that Hazel liked so much.

"He is, actually." Paddy put a hand on the dog's head. "He's my service dog."

"Well, he is a very handsome fellow," Andy said softly. But Hazel could tell her focus had already shifted.

She's nervous. Hazel realized the fact with a jolt of surprise. She scanned Andy's body language again and there, beneath the cool, aloof façade, was the subtle hint of anxiety. It was in the way Andy shifted back and forth in her classy sandals and in the way her jaw tightened. Hazel was surprised to see Darcy's body language mirrored in her great-niece. She'd only seen Darcy nervous once, but the experience had made an impression. Equally intriguing was the discovery that Andy could demonstrate *anything* but confidence.

"Well, we will just take our seats."

"Are you here to bid, Mr. Quinn?"

"Um, no." Paddy smiled. "Just here for the spectacle."

Hazel nodded to Andy, who still seemed ill at ease, and then allowed her father to lead them to seats in the back. They shook hands and greeted neighbors along the way. Hazel was pleased to recognize a few faces she'd not seen for a while. She waved to a reclusive elderly woman and was rewarded with a wave and a nod in return. At last, they sat down beneath the lightly flapping tent in folding chairs. Nubi lay down at their feet, crossed his paws, and propped his chin on them. His golden eyes roamed the crowd, however, never at rest.

Hazel watched as a man angled behind them leaned forward and began speaking softly in Paddy's ear. Cliff Lewis and Paddy had gone to school together and had run around with Paddy's brother Amos back in the day. Her father quirked his lips and then nodded. Hazel turned to look at the woman about her age sitting beside Cliff.

"What do you think about all this?" Raine nodded to where Ernest Hardy was standing by the podium with his hat in his hands.

"I think"—Hazel paused to look at Andy—"that this won't play out the way Mr. Hardy wants."

"That's what I was telling Pa." Raine leaned forward on sinewy forearms. A curl of light brown hair fell forward. She jerked her narrow chin toward Andy. "That hotshot has seriously underestimated us if she thinks we're going to be paying inflated prices for these lots."

"You're bidding?" Hazel turned in her chair to address Raine more fully, her interest piqued.

"Hell, yeah. Lots 1 and 4."

"Ah, for the cattle?"

"And more room for the horses."

"Know of anyone else bidding? I see that Frankie is here." Hazel turned her gaze to the older woman she'd waved to earlier to find her gaze trained toward the podium where Andy stood.

"Nah, my aunt doesn't need any more property. She just doesn't like her news secondhand." Raine squinted at the backs of all their neighbors' heads. "I know Jack and Jake Oglesby are gunning for Lots 2 and 3."

"Yeah, that would be a lot of corn," Hazel murmured as she too scanned the crowd for the brothers. "Lots 5, 6, and 7?"

"No idea." Raine shook her head. "I do know that no one here will be paying one hundred grand for an acre of land."

"Definitely not."

"But I get the sense that's exactly what the Ice Queen is expecting."

Hazel nodded at the characterization as she looked back at Andy. She did fit the part, physically and metaphorically. But Hazel knew this was unfair. Andy wasn't cold. When she had spoken about leaving the courtroom due to burnout, Hazel could tell there was more to it. There had been a flash of personal regret in Andy's eyes. And her quiet insistence that Hazel take Darcy's old aprons. Andy had known they held sentimental value to her. That was not the behavior of an unfeeling person.

"She's actually a decent person. Just…" Hazel frowned as she puzzled for the right word. "She's just unaccustomed to us."

Raine sat back and raised a brow. "You've spent time with her?"

"She lives across the street from me." Hazel laughed.

"Yeah, but…" She looked back at Andy with a frown. After a moment her face cleared, and she grinned at Hazel. "You've *spent time* with her."

Hazel knew what her friend was insinuating and her face flushed. "No. I just helped her install some deadbolts."

"I bet you did."

Hazel couldn't help laughing loudly, causing several heads to turn. Chiefly interested were Paddy and Cliff.

"What's so funny?" Cliff queried in his quiet voice.

"You don't wanna know, Pa," Raine said before Hazel could dispel the suspicion.

Paddy gave his daughter a smile, but Cliff squinted at Raine. "I'm certain you're right, Buster. Forget I asked."

The women grinned at one another as a feminine voice came over the microphone at the front of the tent. The chatter quieted almost at once. Hazel considered that her neighbors must be pretty interested. The noiselessness came upon the crowd more quickly than it did when their pastor began speaking.

Hazel was suddenly hit with an amusing notion of what Darcy would have to say about the crowd. She would accuse her neighbors of being nosy busybodies who were just there for the gossip. Darcy would then have tossed back her head, laughed, and turned to the person next to her for exactly the same reason. The image made Hazel smile.

Andy had removed her sunglasses and was gazing about at the crowd of guarded, but curious faces.

"Greetings. Such a wonderful turnout to our *spectacle*." She smiled and Hazel swore Andy's icy gaze met her eyes. Hazel winked at her just in case. Andy said a few words of welcome in a smooth, cultured voice and then turned over the proceedings to the auctioneer, who immediately began rapidly spitting out numbers.

It seemed they were going to proceed in numerical order. Hazel looked at the program and map in her hands. The price the auctioneer had begun with was preposterous for fourteen acres. Hazel cut her eyes over her shoulder to Raine, who shook her head.

"Come on, folks!" The auctioneer smiled around at everyone. "Y'all planning to spend money or what?" There were a few sympathetic chuckles. "Alright, what about seven hundred thousand five hundred?"

As if this had been the signal Cliff had been waiting for, he turned to Raine. She nodded to him and threw her arm in the air. "Back here!" She threw her voice over the heads of her neighbors.

"Now we're talking!" The auctioneer shouted and then glanced to Andy, who was making a notation in a notebook with a small smile. "How about seven hundred thousand and three quarters?"

But the audience had clammed up once again, and no matter how the auctioneer cajoled them, they would not be moved to bid against Raine and Cliff. With a disappointed sigh, the auctioneer was forced to yell "Sold!" and they moved on to Lot 2.

Each parcel followed suit. Hazel realized her neighbors had made up their mind to bid on only what they needed and only for the price they deemed fair. The auctioneer persuaded, seduced, even shamed them, but they would not be swayed. She did her damnedest to hide her mirth at the situation.

Andy, however, did not seem amused. Before the auction, Hazel had checked the going rate per acre. The first two tracts of land had sold for slightly lower than the market price. It was no wonder Andy looked irritated. As the next few lots went similarly, she looked dejected. When the last tract of property was sold, Andy looked positively defeated. Her body language was subtle, and Hazel was sure no one else would have known the difference, but she could tell from the way she held her shoulders, slightly rounded now, that this had been a humbling blow.

She acknowledged an internal grin as the final purchases were summarized and the crowd dismissed. Still, as funny as the situation was and as proud as Hazel was of her neighbors and their spirit of tenacity and fairness, she couldn't help being sympathetic toward Andy. *I did try to warn her.*

She stood and congratulated Raine and Cliff on their purchase before retreating with her father and Anubis to the edge of the tent. Hazel kept Andy on her peripherals as she seemed to be in a tense discussion with Mr. Hardy. Hazel felt another pang of sympathy. She had not considered that Andy had to answer to her client and that he might be far from happy with the outcome of the auction. Andy was cool and collected as she concluded the discussion and turned her back on Mr. Hardy's red face.

As she turned, Hazel, who had paused to watch the interaction, accidentally caught her eye. A wry grin twisted across Andy's face briefly as she nodded to her and then turned her attention to the auctioneer. It was apparent she had many more uncomfortable conversations to conclude that day and was not looking forward to it.

Once Hazel and Paddy had escaped to the coolness of her vehicle, they turned to one another and smiled.

"Well, that was…" Paddy made a sweeping motion with his hand.

"Something." Hazel shook her head and backed up, turned around in the yard, and headed down the gravel drive. "I feel bad for Andy."

"Me too." He looked over at her. "Changed your tune a bit?" She cut her eyes, but he laughed.

"I never said I wanted her to *fail!*"

"No, but you prescribed a dose of humility, if I remember correctly."

"Well, we can all use a dose of that from time to time."

He shook his head. "Not me. I'm perfect."

Hazel grinned at his mock-serious face. "You're right, Pops. You are perfect."

CHAPTER FIVE

Andy sat down heavily with a glass of bourbon. She kicked off her wingtips and propped her socked feet on the study coffee table. The marred surface of the table reflected just how she felt at the moment. Andy dragged her hand down her face and then took a healthy swig of the liquor, savoring the burn with masochistic relish. She quickly tossed back the rest and reached for the bottle again, marveling at its near emptiness.

Andy had bought the bottle the day of the auction, and it had barely lasted three days. It had been an awful three days. She poured another ration of the dark, warm bourbon and sat back to drink it slowly. After several days of negotiating with the auctioneer and with the understandably irate Ernest Hardy, she could finally put that clusterfuck behind her. She asked herself for the hundredth time what had happened. It should have been gravy. She had done everything just the way it should have been done, and yet the community of Green Valley had thwarted her.

Hazel had warned her. And she had dismissed Hazel casually. Andy knew there was an inevitable reckoning coming. She needed help. She needed to get into the community if she was going to be successful here. And Andy was determined to be successful. There was no reality in which she could return to Birmingham with her tail between her legs.

The evening after the auction she'd come home, turned off her phone, and thrown herself into the bottle of bourbon. It wasn't a healthy coping mechanism, but it had gotten her through the night. The next morning, after facing her demons, she had been determined to make it work in Green Valley. She had come here for a fresh start, and she had nowhere to go but up from her current position.

Just as she had taken another sip of her bourbon, the power flickered once, twice, and then went out. Andy frowned and stood up in the semi-dark. She had been vaguely aware of the wind and darkening clouds when she'd let herself into the house but had been too preoccupied to care. Lightning flashed and illuminated a path to the windows in the corner. Andy peered out only to be blinded by a brilliant bolt of electricity. The wind lashed the rain against the windowpanes with a wet staccato.

In the darkness, the room seemed far lonelier than usual. She turned on her phone's flashlight and padded into the front parlor to look out of the bay window. Through the rain and the green-black of the wet magnolia leaves, Andy could see the lights on at Hazel's house.

"What the hell?" Looking left and right, she realized Hazel must have a generator. The gloom around her suddenly felt oppressive. "Ah, what the hell." She retrieved a brand new, squeaky pair of Wellington boots she had special-ordered for the inevitability of just this occasion.

Andy donned her rain slicker before slipping her feet into the still stiff boots. This was the first time she had worn them, and a rubbery smell wafted up to her nostrils. The scent somehow emboldened her, and she pulled up the hood of her slicker, unearthed a flashlight from the heavy table in the foyer, and went out into the night.

❖

Hazel was surprised by a knock on her door. She thought she'd heard heavy footsteps on her front porch steps, but had assumed it was thunder. A jacketed form stood at the glass and, after a pause, shook back a hood to reveal silver-blond hair.

"I'll be," Hazel murmured with a bemused smile. She welcomed Andy Richter across her threshold.

"Hi."

"Hi." Hazel smiled. "Nice night for a stroll."

Andy didn't blush exactly, but her face and neck did take on a deeper color. "I thought so." She hung the rain slicker on the coat rack and dropped her squelching boots just outside the door. They clunked solidly against the porch boards. "My power went out," Andy explained as she turned back to Hazel.

"I see. And you came here because I have a genny."

"No." Andy shook her head, then paused. "Well, partly. I came here because I wanted to speak with you, and the power going out persuaded me that I had nothing better to do."

"Than speak with me? I'm flattered."

Andy huffed in an impatient sort of way. "No. I'm bumbling."

"Have you had dinner?" Hazel took pity on Andy. She knew damn well why Andy had come, and it was suddenly important to Hazel that she serve Andy something better than crow.

Andy frowned. "No, I haven't."

"Come. Sit at the bar." Hazel gestured to the island and stools. "I'll make something…Do you like grilled cheese?"

Finally, Andy smiled and seemed to release a breath. "Who doesn't like grilled cheese?"

"My thoughts exactly." Hazel busied herself with gathering ingredients from the fridge to allow Andy a moment to compose herself once again.

When she turned back around, Andy's cool gaze was on her, but it seemed thoughtful rather than cold as it usually did.

"I came to tell you that I should have listened," Andy said without preamble, and met her eyes directly. "You were right."

Hazel smiled into the intense gaze. Her estimation of Andy jumped exponentially. She'd known this was the true nature of Andy's visit, but for Andy to address it so directly and without excuse impressed Hazel a great deal.

"Thank you for your straightforwardness, Andy. I was going to feed you anyway."

Andy laughed and Hazel experienced a small thrill knowing she could entertain the usually stoic woman.

"Well, I'd rather be safe about it." She leaned forward, planting her forearms on the island.

"You look like Darcy when you're nervous," Hazel said on impulse.

Andy tilted her head. "Do I? How so?"

"She used to tighten her jaw and shift back and forth. She would get fidgety. Or at least that was the way she acted when Horace got sick."

"Horace?" Andy frowned. "Horace was a close friend?"

Hazel grinned at the characterization of Darcy's mule. It was more accurate than Andy could have known. "Something like that." Hazel changed the subject. "Did you lose a lot of money at the auction?"

"Not too much." Andy sighed. "Luckily, I had money set aside for a bust or two."

Hazel poured the leftover tomato soup from a food storage

container into a saucepan and placed it on the gas burner before constructing the grilled cheese sandwiches.

"That's not lucky," she said and again met Andy's eyes. "That's good planning."

"I suppose you know a few things about that, being a landlord yourself?"

"I always keep something squirreled away." Hazel slipped a pad of butter into the heated skillet. The sizzling filled the quiet between the women as they watched it turn to liquid in the pan. Hazel placed the first sandwich into the pan carefully and covered it with an aluminum melting dome.

"There's a whole process to these sandwiches."

"Of course there is." Hazel stirred the soup. "Now, where do you go from here? What's the plan?"

Andy sighed. "I need to know this community. No…" She paused. "I need to be *a part* of this community. And I need your help for that."

Hazel found the idea of leading Andy out into society amusing. *Like a debutante.* She smiled at the image. "How would you like to begin?"

Andy shook her head. "I was hoping *you* would have ideas about that."

"Hmm…" Hazel considered the upcoming calendar. "Well, there's a local fishing competition in a few days. Every-one is bound to be there."

"A fishing competition?"

"Yes, like Bassmaster, but country. My dad and Uncle Amos always take their boat out. I usually take a kayak. I have a spare." *Oh, but perhaps Andy has never been in a kayak.*

"I love to kayak." Andy laughed as though she'd read Hazel's mind. "I'm a city girl, but I'm not totally inept."

Hazel laughed and flipped the grilled cheese before covering it once again with the dome. "I wasn't judging."

Andy looked at her and tilted her head. "You really weren't, were you?" She spoke softly and with a note of wonder in her voice. "You don't know how rare that is."

"I have bad qualities, too."

Andy laughed again and Hazel knew she would never tire of the sound. "Something to drink?"

"I wouldn't mind some of your lemonade."

"I've got plenty." Hazel couldn't explain why she was so pleased Andy enjoyed the lemonade. It didn't matter at the moment, however. She poured the liquid and placed the glass near Andy's right hand.

"Does your father live here, too?"

"He lives in a tiny house in the side yard. It's not ideal as far as space goes, but it works. He did live across town, but once the Parkinson's started to progress, we moved him closer."

"I suppose this arrangement preserves his dignity and autonomy while allowing you to check in with him?"

"That's it exactly." Hazel didn't know how to explain how much she appreciated that Andy got it. She withdrew the first sandwich and added the second one to the pan with liberal amounts of butter.

"And he has Anubis. Nubi," she said with a smile.

"He does, and he also has friends that pick him up and take him places. Amos and Cliff."

"Cliff Lewis?"

"Yes, he and Dad have been friends since high school."

Andy quietly stared at the tomato soup, which had begun a sluggish, slow bubbling. "Mr. Lewis has a daughter, correct?"

This slight pivot caused Hazel to look up at Andy sharply. She couldn't place Andy's tone. "Yes, her name is Raine. Well," Hazel amended, "*Lorraine* is actually her name, but she goes by Raine."

"I see." Andy raised her brows. "Tall drink of water, isn't she?"

Hazel frowned at first. Unsure as to what Andy meant with her suggestive tone. "I guess." As Andy continued to smirk, it dawned on Hazel to what Andy was alluding. "I mean, I've known her forever, so…" She shrugged and then busied herself checking on the grilled cheese to hide her uncertainty about what to say.

"So, you *haven't* dated her?"

Hazel's face was suddenly warm She scolded herself for her reaction, which only made it worse. "N-no," she said as firmly as she could muster. "What makes you think I would want to?"

Andy tilted her head again, her chin-length hair swinging to one side and catching the glimmer of the lights above the island. "I'm sorry." She sat back on the stool and looked Hazel over with wide eyes. "I suppose being out is difficult in such a rural place."

A bit of sweat trickled down the back of Hazel's neck below her loose, low ponytail. The grilled cheese continued to sizzle as she stepped away from the stove and toward the fridge for a glass of water.

She just needed one moment to collect herself as she decided how to approach the conversation. A furtive glance in Andy's direction told Hazel that Andy was completely at ease and, even worse, expecting an answer.

"No, I'm not out. I've never needed to be."

"Interesting." Andy leaned forward again.

Hazel searched for judgment in the tone of Andy's voice but found none. Her stiff back relaxed somewhat. Flipping the grilled cheese onto a plate and ladling soup into ceramic bowls, Hazel passed Andy the meal.

"Any relationships I've had have been out of town."

"I'm sorry for springing the question on you. I wasn't trying to make you uncomfortable."

Hazel smiled, and more of the tension lessened. "I believe that. No need to apologize. I just don't consider my love life to be of much interest to people."

Andy chuckled. "I think you're mistaken there."

"How's that?"

"Raine Lewis is definitely interested." Andy took a delicate sip of her drink; the ice tinkled in the silence between them.

"Um, I don't think so." Hazel shook her head. *God, why is it so hot in here?* She glared at the thermostat across the room though she knew damned well that wasn't the problem.

"I do. She watched you during the auction like you were a verdant tract of land."

A part of Hazel knew this was probably true. Raine had always been incredibly attentive to her. Chivalrous, even, but—

"I'm not interested in Raine Lewis."

"Because she's local?"

"Because she's Raine."

"That bad, is she?"

Hazel winced and looked at Andy's smile. She knew Andy was teasing, but she didn't want to give her the wrong impression. "No, Raine is a wonderful person. Hardworking, funny, loyal, but she's just not what I'm looking for." Hazel watched Andy carefully break a piece from the grilled cheese and struggle silently with the strings of cheese that seemed reluctant to separate from the rest of the sandwich. "Are you interested in Raine?"

"Me?" Andy chuckled again. "No, not my usual type."

Hazel saw an opportunity to take revenge on Andy for her teasing tone. "What is your type, then, Andy Richter?"

Andy smirked and wiped her mouth, running one napkinned finger around the perimeter of her quirked lips. Hazel followed the finger with her eyes, mesmerized. She snapped out of it as Andy spoke.

"Woman is my type."

Ugh. Hazel rolled her eyes. "So, you're a player?"

Andy narrowed her eyes. "Not at all. I think you misunderstand. Not all women are my type."

"You're right, I don't understand." Hazel laughed and took a less than delicate bite of her food. She savored the rosemary she had gotten just right in this batch of soup.

"It's not about a type necessarily," Andy said. "It's about how a woman carries herself. I like women who have opinions, hobbies, and careers. I like women who know who they are. Successful women. I also typically like people more on the feminine side of the gender expression spectrum. Which rules Raine out."

Andy's tastes were sophisticated. Of course they were. She must have misunderstood the suggestive glances thrown her way. She was disappointed and embarrassed.

"You'll be hard-pressed to find women like that around here."

Andy frowned. "Why is that?"

Hazel let out a mirthless bark of laughter. "Not many accomplished, professional sophisticates in Green Valley."

The lines between Andy's brows deepened. "I don't believe that's what I said."

"That's the impression you gave."

"Maybe you're projecting." Andy wiped her fingers on her napkin. "Maybe an accomplished professional is what *you're* looking for."

"Perhaps. Would you happen to know one?" Hazel asked teasingly, but Andy's face suddenly shut down.

"Not anymore," she said quietly and took the last bite of her grilled cheese before pushing the plate away. "Thank you for your generosity and your grace, Hazel."

Hazel was wrong-footed by the sudden switch of gears but smiled and nodded. "Should I pick you up for the fishing tournament?"

Andy brightened slightly as she looked round at her once more. "How about I walk over around six and help you strap on the kayaks?"

At *strap on*, Hazel narrowed her eyes slightly. She was unsure if Andy was messing with her. Andy's face did seem a little too casual, but Hazel wasn't certain if the phrase was deliberate.

"Make it seven and I'll make coffee."

"It's a deal." Andy rose from her seat and looked toward the darkened window. "It looks as though the rain has slowed."

"Good. Your walk back won't be so wet."

Andy took her jacket and opened the door. "I don't mind wet," she said over her shoulder with an arched brow and stepped out into the night.

Hazel stared after her. Whatever Andy said, she walked and talked like a player. "'The lady doth protest too much, methinks,'" she said to the empty room.

With a shake of her head, she rounded the island and disposed of the scraps in the garbage. Hazel loaded the dishwasher and wiped down her countertops. She felt more settled once everything was back in place. Andy could push her blood pressure to a peak quicker than anyone she'd ever known. And with such nonchalance! They'd simply been having a conversation and Hazel had blushed like a fool.

She frowned as she put honey, a sprig of mint, and a plain black tea bag in her cup and put the kettle on. The comforting *click, click, whoosh* of the stove eye did an incredible amount more to settle her jangled nerves. As she waited for the water to boil, she mulled over what Andy had said about Raine.

She'd known about Raine's affection, honestly. It had always been there in the background of their relationship. It was one of the reasons Hazel avoided spending too much time alone with Raine. She didn't want to give her the wrong idea, and dating around town would lead to complications she couldn't face. Complications she wasn't *willing* to face.

She did not know how her father would react to her being out. He wouldn't be unkind, but Hazel didn't want to put herself in the position to be at odds with him. Or the rest of town, for that matter. It just wasn't worth it. She liked the way things were. They weren't necessarily exciting, but they were comfortable, and that was just fine.

But she had several reasons for not dating Raine, regardless of how wonderful she was. Hazel simply wasn't interested. There just wasn't a spark there like there was with—

She jumped when the tea kettle began its slow whine and turned off the eye before the kettle could reach its vaporous crescendo. As she poured the water into the teacup, it sizzled. Hazel placed a tea cake on the saucer and stepped onto the porch.

The smell of wet, green life hit her nose, and she inhaled deeply. She placed the cup and saucer on the side table and sat in her favorite rocking chair. The creak of the rocker couldn't drown out the percussion of the cicadas nor the thrumming resonance of the bullfrogs. Thunder persisted in the distance, and the clouds shuddered and trembled with illumination from occasional lightning. The brilliance reflected across the sky, contrasting starkly with the glistening darkness and leaving an imprint of the clouds and skyline in her mind. The film-negative image came and went so swiftly that when Hazel closed her eyes to try to hold on to the vision, it was like trying to grasp the details of a vague dream.

She brought her teacup to her lips and, as she did so, remembered Andy's. Her lips weren't particularly full or pouty. They weren't brightly painted or adorably bow-shaped. Despite all of this, she couldn't call to mind a sexier mouth. The way Andy smirked, with one side quirked up, was captivating. Her smile was reserved but not reluctant. Hazel couldn't get it out of her mind. Deep down, she didn't want to.

CHAPTER SIX

A ndy awoke a few days later wondering why her alarm was sounding so early. When she realized it was the day of the fishing tournament, she smiled and rose from bed with alacrity. She loved kayaking and she greatly enjoyed Hazel's company. Andy pictured the heated blush on Hazel's face. It had erupted from her neck and effused her face with radiance. So lovely. Andy savored the image and longed to be the cause of such a flush again, and again, and again…

Pushing these thoughts aside, she set about her morning routine. The black, one-piece swimming suit she had ordered online fit well. Over this, she pulled a V-neck tee and a pair of lightweight cropped pants before topping her head with a dry-fit ball cap. Andy tightened her strappy sandals, grabbed her canvas cross-bag, and was downstairs and out the door.

She stepped down the worn but sturdy steps of the front porch and set out across the yard. Once she reached the magnolias that flanked the drive, she could see Hazel wrestling with a bright blue kayak. A yellow one lay on the ground beside her green Subaru. Hazel nearly had the blue one mounted when it slipped sideways, and she hopped back to avoid it crushing her toes. Andy could hear her cursing from the road and smiled.

Andy was going to call out to remind Hazel she had offered to help, but as she approached, Andy became distracted by the view. She admired the way Hazel's short cotton skirt flared around her full hips and the curve of her backside as she reached over her head in the second attempt at mounting the kayak. It was too easy to imagine running her fingertips down the outside of Hazel's legs or grabbing handfuls of her—

"Oh! Good morning!" Hazel said exuberantly. "I just got the first one up, but I'd prefer help with the second."

Andy pulled her attention back to Hazel's flushed face. "As I recall, I offered help with the first one as well."

"You did, but—"

"I'll load this one, then." Andy stepped forward before Hazel could protest and deftly lifted the kayak onto the roof rack of the wagon. Her long arms afforded her the ability to reach the ties on either end. After a minute of pushing, pulling, and wiggling, the kayak was loaded.

"You made that look easy."

"Next time, you'll let me help." Andy glossed over the fact that she assumed there would be a next time and instead pointed to the porch. "You promised coffee."

Hazel grinned.

❖

Andy looked at Hazel questioningly as she turned off the main road. Hazel must have felt the scrutiny because she glanced at her.

"It will be too crowded to park at the boat ramp. We're going to put in at a little spring-fed creek that runs into the lake. It's close to where the competition begins. From there, we can find Dad and Uncle Amos on their boat." Hazel looked directly at her for a moment. Andy saw Hazel scan her body. "Not that you'll be concerned, but we will need to carry the kayaks a short distance."

"Now you tell me?" Andy heard her voice light, full of wry humor.

Hazel grinned and shrugged before fiddling with the strap of her swimming suit top beneath her loose, sleeveless shirt. "Are you saying you can't handle the strain?"

Andy raised a brow and bit back a chuckle, but she purred on the inside. Rather than answering immediately, she settled back into her seat, careful to flex her quads and forearms as she did so. "I think you'll find that I'm quite accustomed to strain and not at all deterred by it."

"Is that so?"

Unless she was much mistaken, Hazel's breathing had quickened slightly. "Yes, it is. Do you require an exhibition?"

"Ah, no, that's alright."

"Are you certain? I've found there's nothing quite like hands-on experience to demonstrate a point." Andy enjoyed the effect her words had on Hazel. She was definitely breathing more rapidly through her nose as though trying to control the pace of her lungs. That gorgeous flush was creeping up her neck and face again.

"I'm sure." Hazel cleared her throat and changed the subject. "Did you bring a drybag?"

"I have a small one folded in here." Andy pointed to the cross-body bag on the floorboard of the vehicle. "Just big enough for my phone and some sunscreen. Will that do?"

"Perfect. I have a spare, but I should have known you would be prepared."

"I don't like surprises."

Hazel glanced over with a grin. "No? The last time you were surprised, was it really that bad?"

"That auction."

"Okay…besides that."

"You're changing the terms of the game."

"God, you're such a lawyer."

Andy laughed out loud this time. "Guilty as charged."

Hazel made a face. "Ugh, what a pun." Her eyes were fixed, sweeping the road, seemingly in search of something. "Hold that thought, here we are." She steered the wagon gently to a fence and cattle gate. "I'll be right back." She slipped out of the car and opened the gate so that they could drive through into the pasture. Hazel closed the gate and returned to the vehicle.

"We're not trespassing, are we?"

"If we were?"

"I know that people out here shoot first and ask questions later."

The car bumped along so that when Hazel chuckled, it came out in bursts of alternating volume. "True. But we're not trespassing. This pasture is part of a larger estate that was farmed for a long time, but not since Mr. Parson passed away. Mrs. Parson loaned me a key to the padlock so that I could put my kayak in at Percy Creek. She knows that I come and go out here."

"It seems like a long way to go to kayak."

"I also forage out here from time to time. This is one of the last natural reserves in the county. It's pretty untouched, so I know what I'm harvesting is in good health."

"So, these people don't mind that you're taking stuff from their land?"

Hazel put the car in park and looked across the console

at her. "I've known the Parsons my whole life. Mr. and Mrs. Parson didn't have any children. No family to work the farm or see to the cattle. I always got the impression that they were just glad someone was enjoying the property responsibly."

Andy found that it made sense, but only in a Green Valley way. There were not many natural, green spaces in Birmingham. The only thing she could conjure that was similar was the Botanical Gardens. But that was public land. They were on private property.

"I guess you hope someone with your mindset inherits the property."

Hazel paused in the act of checking the contents of her drybag. "What do you mean?"

"You said they didn't have kids." Andy shrugged. "I guess it would be best for you if the property goes to someone else in their family. Someone you know." She gestured out the window at the rolling pastureland and the tree line. "So this will stay the same."

Hazel looked around. "I try not to think about that." She exited the car.

Andy followed suit and looked at her over the top of the Subaru. "I didn't mean to bring down the mood."

Hazel smiled. "You didn't. Tomorrow can take care of itself. Let's go kayaking today."

Andy returned the smile and then surveyed her surroundings. It was shaping up to be a scorching day. She was glad she had packed sunscreen and a hat. The azure sky shone brilliantly, crossed only briefly by high, wispy clouds. There was no hint of the storm that had taken out her power only a few days before.

The smell of the sun-drenched grass in the pasture hit her. It was sweet and sharp and filled her lungs to capacity. Andy had the urge to lie in it, to hide herself in its tall, raspy depths.

Shaking this bizarre idea away, she aided Hazel in retrieving the kayaks.

They laid them side by side with enough room between the tough polyethylene hulls for them to stand. Andy moved to the back and gestured to the nylon rope handles. "I'll follow you."

Hazel nodded and stepped before her. They bent simultaneously and lifted the boats easily. Andy timed her longer steps with Hazel's shorter stride so as to not jostle the rhythm of their progress. She followed Hazel to the edge of the pasture and into the tree line where cool, mossy shade prickled her skin. The sensation was a stark contrast to the warmth of the shining field.

Hazel slowed and jerked her head toward a gently sloped, somewhat sandy bank in a wide, shallow creek. Andy nodded to the back of Hazel's head on reflex, then, remembering Hazel couldn't see her, cleared her throat.

"Understood." She lowered the boats. She was sweating but not out of breath and was pleased to see neither was Hazel. Her companion was no stranger to strain either.

They slid the boats into the water, and Hazel stepped unhesitatingly into the creek before turning back. "Now, the water is—"

"Freezing!" Andy gasped as she too had strode directly into the water up to her calves. The silted bottom of the creek had given way beneath her sandals, and she was forced to throw out an arm to keep her balance. The cold had shocked her. This was June!

Hazel laughed loudly. The kaleidoscope of the green canopy overhead swallowed the sound. "We're literally twenty feet from the mouth of a spring. The water is cold here year-round." She bent down, cupped her hands, and splashed the frigid water over her face and chest.

Andy watched her pluck in amazement. Her eyes followed the path of the water as it sluiced down Hazel's neck and disappeared into her ample cleavage. Andy shook her head and tugged the blue kayak farther out into the creek before slipping in as smoothly as she could manage. The bending of her knees to accommodate her length in the boat caused cold rivulets of water to run along the underside of her thighs. She wiped them away briskly and tried not to focus on how the cold water would feel running along her arms as she dipped and raised the paddle.

Hazel was already in her boat waiting a few yards away. She seemed completely at ease as she sat with her face tilted to the sun filtering through the trees. Tendrils of her brown hair had already escaped from her French braid, and they framed her face in delicate whisps.

Come on, Richter, cowboy up. She dipped her paddle and propelled forward easily. The smooth glide of the boat along the creek was immensely satisfying and she smiled at Hazel. "I'm ready."

"Great. We'll just follow the creek about half a mile. It will spit us out near where the boats put in earlier this morning." Hazel checked a sports watch on her wrist that Andy hadn't seen her wear before. "We shouldn't have any issue with traffic. Everything officially started at six, so we should be clear."

"And you said Amos and Paddy will have their own boat?"

"Yes, a massive pontoon boat. Everyone stops by for a visit at some point, so there's really no telling who all will be there when we pull alongside." Hazel looked over her shoulder and smiled.

"More surprises." Andy reminded herself that mingling with the community was what she wanted. It was the whole reason for being in this cold creek in the first place. Hazel's lovely face looked back at her and Andy amended her thought. The *main* reason, anyway.

Hazel laughed. "Have you *never* had a good surprise?"

Andy considered the question as she paddled along the sun dappled creek.

"Finding out I inherited my great-aunt's estate was a pleasant surprise."

"Yeah? How did that come about?"

There was an odd note in Hazel's voice that Andy couldn't place. She remembered Hazel had been close to Aunt Darcy and continued with this in mind.

"I'm still not certain. My father's father, George, was Darcy's younger brother. He's the one who left Green Valley for Birmingham. From what I can tell, he never really looked back. It wasn't until my grandmother passed that my dad had anything to do with Darcy. He was young when it happened. Grandpa George was at a loss, and so he began sending Dad here during the summers." Andy paused to pluck some weeds from her paddle. "Darcy made an impact on Dad, but we didn't visit much. He was a defense attorney and always very busy. I didn't know Darcy that well, so I was surprised I received the estate when she passed."

"You think she did it for your dad? What did he think?"

Andy shrugged. "I really don't know. Like I said, I didn't know Darcy. As for what Dad thought, I don't know that either. He passed a few years ago."

"I'm sorry for your loss," Hazel said, and she really did sound it.

Andy jerked her head in acknowledgment. "I'm sorry for yours. The word around town is that Darcy was a hell of a person. You two were obviously close. I wish I'd had the opportunity to know her." As she said it, Andy realized a twinge of regret. She meant it. Everyone she'd spoken to about Darcy gushed about her. Andy had missed an important opportunity and was sorry for it.

Hazel glanced back with a smile. "She really was an extraordinary person." There was a bend in the creek, and they didn't speak as they navigated the gentle curve. "I did know Darcy well." Hazel resumed the conversation. "And I remember her speaking fondly of her summers with your father. I understand why she left you the property. She was very sentimental."

"I'm not so much."

"I have noticed. Which raises the question: Why move out here? Why not just sell the house?"

Andy paused, measuring her words. The lush undergrowth of the woods slipped by on the bank, cool and green and refreshing. She could smell the silt and the mud and scrutinized the ripples created by a large, flat-looking turtle where it silently slipped into the water from a sunny rock.

Andy was unfamiliar with the process of freely sharing her thoughts and feelings. As a result, she was undecided as to how much to disclose about her exodus from Birmingham and her life of criminal defense. Part of this *new beginning* was being more open. Hazel seemed like a safe person to share with, and she liked the way Hazel looked at her. But Andy didn't want to say anything that would diminish her in Hazel's opinion. She decided to start slowly and then see how it went.

"I was running away," Andy said. *So much for starting slow.* "Professionally, I mean." She tried to backpedal.

"Running away from being a defense attorney?" Hazel's tone was curious.

Andy relaxed a knot of tension in her shoulders. "Yes. My client was a corrupt cop, and the leading witness—the one that could have put him away—turned up dead."

"Killed?"

"It looked like a standard mugging, but she'd been—" Andy faltered. It had been a grisly scene. She'd seen the photos. "She was killed in a way that pointed back to my client."

"Wait." Hazel turned slowly. "I think I read about this in the news."

Ice slipped into Andy's stomach. "You probably did."

"The woman was garroted."

Andy forced herself to breathe slowly and steadily through her nose. "Yes. It was gruesome. It couldn't be tied to the police officer, but it was too coincidental for it not to be his doing. He had that woman killed so that he could walk free. The case was dismissed." *As though the witness had meant nothing.*

"I'm sorry that happened," Hazel said softly. "I understand your need to put some distance between you and that situation." They paddled around another bend. "Do you think you would ever return to law?"

Andy frowned. She hadn't had the courage to ask herself that yet. "I'm not certain. I turned my back on that life, that world. I needed a clean break."

"That makes sense. But I think you were wrong."

"What?" Andy's heart plummeted. The thought that she had ruined whatever this thing was between them by sharing her past made her queasy.

"Yes, you began by saying you had run away. As though you're some sort of coward. I think you're very brave to try to reinvent yourself."

A strange warmth spread over Andy as she took Hazel's words in. Before she could reply, however, they came around another bend and suddenly, the bank was on fire. Tall, spindly stalks with clusters of bright red flowers were standing like candles along the edge of the water.

"What are those?" Andy was amazed by the sight.

"Cardinal flowers. They're actually pretty rare. This is the only spot in the county I've found them growing like this."

"I've never seen them before. They almost glow."

Hazel back-paddled and Andy came abreast of her. Hazel looked across the clear, cool creek and pinned Andy with those amber eyes. Andy sensed she was being measured.

"That's exactly what I thought when I first saw them."

"We have the lilies in Birmingham. Have you seen them?"

"The Cahaba lilies? No, I haven't."

"They're beautiful. White and sharp and asserting themselves against the will of the river." Andy turned again to the cardinal flowers. "Why are the cardinal flowers rare?"

"Over-picking, mostly. And they're poisonous, so farmers don't want them around."

"Makes sense. But they are beautiful." Andy looked to Hazel once more. "How much farther to the lake?"

"Just around the bend."

❖

They found Amos and Paddy with little difficulty. Hazel knew where they usually dropped anchor, but the cluster of assorted boats anchored around the pontoon acted like a neon sign. She and Andy hadn't spoken much once they'd hit the lake, as kayaking on the larger body of water was more difficult than in the small creek. Hazel mulled over what Andy had told her.

She had read an article about the murder of the witness. The word *garroted* flashed through her mind again. *Poor Andy.* That must have been quite a shock. Hazel knew she would have been absolutely sick if it had been her job to defend that sort of person. She could tell Andy felt terrible about it. Hazel wondered exactly what all she had walked away from when she had moved to Green Valley.

Tucking these ruminations away, she pulled her kayak alongside the pontoon boat, and Amos cast her a rope and carabiner to clip to the kayak's handle. Getting out of the kayak was tricky, but she was able to maintain her balance to clamber onto the boat and turn to help Andy manage the feat as well.

"You've done that before," Andy said with an accusatory note in her voice.

Hazel winked. "You handled it well enough."

Andy arched a brow but was immediately accosted by Amos, who welcomed her onto the boat and introduced her to the others sitting about on the vinyl cushions. Hazel kissed her dad on the cheek and sat down beside him. He rummaged in the cooler and pulled out a bottle of gin. Hazel laughed and kissed him again before grabbing a Solo cup and mixing a gin and tonic.

His own drink in hand, Paddy nudged her leg and gestured to a short man in conversation with Amos at the bow of the boat. "Do you remember Barney now?"

Hazel took a closer look, and recognition did dawn on her. "Yes, now I do. He's got that Parson nose, doesn't he?"

Her father grinned. "He does. In school we called him Bozo Barney."

"Pops!" Hazel pretended to be scandalized.

He laughed. "Terrible, isn't it?"

Hazel looked the man over again and shook her head. "Teenagers are all mean to each other. I'm sure you all had awful nicknames for each other."

"Want to know what they used to call Amos?" Paddy winked.

"I think I can guess."

Paddy hooted and Hazel joined in the laughter. It was good to be among her community with a cold drink after a hard paddle. She admired the view of the sparkling water and the dark green foliage on the distant, scattered islands.

The lake was a lively setting. The occasional boat or Jet Ski sped by, leaving the pontoon to absorb the wake with a gentle, undulating motion. The vessel was currently packed full of locals. Most were milling about, bragging about the fish caught that year and in years past. There were numerous coolers and snacks being passed around and a small knot of life-vested kids splashing near the bow of the boat.

Despite the gaiety and hubbub, something was missing. After a moment of looking around, Hazel realized she felt Darcy's absence acutely. Darcy was often in the thick of things, dispensing Solo cups and keeping a steely eye on any kids in the water. A poignant memory surfaced of Darcy vaulting the port side of the pontoon to dive after a kid who had slipped from his life vest. Hazel could not have been more than seven or eight at the time and had been astounded at the swift demonstration of athleticism and determination.

Hazel smiled at the memory but felt a now familiar twinge in her chest at the loss of her friend. Shaking her head to surface from her despair, she automatically scanned the group for Andy. She was in conversation with Cliff Lewis. The tall, wiry man was gesticulating in the empty air between them. She overheard a mention of horses. Perhaps he was describing his plan for the land he'd bought at the auction. To her credit, Andy looked completely at ease and invested in the conversation as though this man hadn't just been part of a great disappointment for her.

This preoccupation with Cliff gave Hazel a few moments to study Andy. She'd not had a proper look at her all morning, and so Hazel made up for lost time and drank her in. Andy stood holding a drink, her sinewy arm muscles flexed and glistening in the unadulterated sunshine. Her legs were still encased in the lightweight cropped pants, but Hazel could just make out the definition of her quads. How could she be so sexy just standing there? Hazel couldn't ignore the low, insistent tug in her belly. There was a primitive part of her that yearned for the weight of Andy between her thighs. Preferably, grinding smoothly as she wrapped her in those muscular arms. And that smartass mouth! Hazel could think of plenty of uses for that...

Suddenly, Andy turned and looked at her. Hazel blushed and looked away. When she looked back, Cliff had Andy's attention once more, but the damn woman was smirking.

Shit. Hazel scolded herself for being so terribly obvious. She took a sip of her drink.

"How was your paddle on the creek? Andy manage the lake okay? She looks fit enough."

"Hmm?" Hazel hid in her cup. How was her drink nearly gone? "Oh, yeah, I guess she's pretty fit. She did fine on both parts of the paddle."

"You look a bit warm. You don't want to take a dip?"

Hazel's first instinct was to say no, but after a pause, she decided a swim might be just what she needed.

"Yeah." She stood and pulled her top over her head. "I think I will." She drained her cup, shucked the cotton skirt over her lilac high-rise bikini bottoms and stepped to the back deck of the pontoon. Without a glance to the rest of the boat, she dove in.

The sudden cocoon of dark, cold water was a mercy to her blushing face and neck. She had arched smoothly to create a shallow dive, and her head broke the tension of the surface quickly. Hazel reveled in the sensation of the green water gliding over her heated skin and quickly dove under once more to linger beneath the surface. Submerged in a quiet, weightless limbo, she was able to settle her embarrassment.

When she broke the surface again, she heard a splash. Hazel wiped the water from her eyes, wondering who had joined her. She was shocked to see Andy's head break the surface of the water twenty feet from her.

"Why do you look so surprised?" Andy struck out in a flawless breaststroke toward her.

Hazel blushed again as she tread water. She shrugged as best as she could while staying afloat. "You looked deep in conversation with Cliff."

"Is that all?" Andy was now at arm's length from her. "Or was it that you didn't expect a city girl to dive into a lake?"

She'd been found out. "I think we could categorize this as a *good* surprise."

Andy raked back her hair. She looked like a sleek, blond seal. Water dripped down her long, thin nose and her eyes sparkled with mirth. "I'm trying to decide if I'm offended."

"Have I not surprised you even once?" Hazel watched her.

Andy smirked. "You're pretty predictable."

Hazel wasn't sure what made her do it. Maybe it was Andy's dismissive tone. Or her mocking smile. Or that she'd had enough of Andy's ribbing. Regardless of the cause and heedless of consequences, she lunged across the short space between them and dunked Andy with force.

Hazel just glimpsed a pair of shocked blue eyes before Andy sank beneath the water. She released her shoulders and swam back a few strokes. Andy popped up, shaking water from her eyes and nose like a startled dog. She gasped for air and glared at Hazel as she caught her breath.

"You're going to regret that, Hazel Quinn."

Hazel smiled broadly and laughed. "You deserved it."

"I disagree." Andy was rapidly regaining her composure

and her eyes sparkled with mischief. She inched forward in the water, but Hazel was not going to be caught unawares.

She backed up just enough for the movement to not be considered a retreat. "You keep your hands to yourself."

Andy held her arms aloft with an arch of her brow. Water sparkled in diamond rivers down her forearms. "Of course." She continued to tread water and move incrementally nearer.

Hazel watched her warily. "Stop creeping up—" Hazel was cut off when Andy leaned back in the water.

The smooth, strong muscles of Andy's legs encircled Hazel's waist, and Hazel had just enough time to take a breath before she was dragged down. The sensation of being beneath Andy in the water was simultaneously thrilling and frightening. Almost as soon as she'd pulled her under, though, Andy's hands were on her upper arms, bringing her back to the surface. Andy held her as she wiped the water from her face and swept her sopping and disheveled braid over her shoulder.

"Fuck you," Hazel grumbled, but didn't move from Andy's capable arms. They were chest to chest, and Hazel could feel the smooth glide of Andy's skin along her stomach and thighs.

Andy laughed loud and triumphantly. "You started it."

"I did not!" Hazel looked into her eyes and was suddenly overwhelmed by how intimate their proximity was. She pushed off from Andy playfully and turned to watch a boat tooling by. She could feel the emotion shining brightly on her face. "Okay, maybe I did, but you deserved that dunk."

The knowing smile on Andy's face did nothing to dispel the knot of pleasant tension that had settled in Hazel's gut.

"I'll admit to nothing."

Hazel had the urge to dunk her again. Instead, she paddled backward to put more space between them. "You're such a lawyer!"

Andy's smile broadened. "We've already established this. I have other qualities, too."

"Other qualities?" Hazel repeated dubiously.

"Other skills."

"Hmm..." *Can you catch fire in a lake?* Hazel was saved from having to retort, however, by a call from her father.

"Come on back in, y'all two! They're wrapping up the competition!" He motioned for them to return to the boat.

Andy turned back to Hazel. "After you."

"No, ma'am, I don't think so."

Andy chuckled and began a smooth, perfect backstroke to the pontoon, keeping her eyes on Hazel during her return. Hazel glared but followed at a safe distance, of course.

CHAPTER SEVEN

Andy opened the creaking cellar doors and fumbled for the light. A single bulb with a string hung in the middle of the ceiling. She reached up and pulled it gingerly, half-afraid it would shock her. It clicked on matter-of-factly and illuminated the cellar. The light drove the shadows to the corners, but did not reach deeper within the dim, cavern-like space. Andy switched on her flashlight and swung the arc of light around the gloom, trying to gauge how much work was in store.

There was a wine rack in the back covered in dust. Andy wasn't sure *what* she would find there. She suspected the wine had turned to vinegar but resolved to begin with the canned goods. There were at least six six-foot shelves of the jars to peruse.

Andy wasn't certain what she would do with all of it just yet. Throwing it away seemed a total waste, but she didn't want to *give* it away and cause anyone to fall ill. She had decided to separate it into stacks based on the year and type, but when she approached the shelves, she realized it had all been organized in this exact way. *That's convenient.*

Andy began moving jars to the cardboard boxes she had stacked on the steps on her way into the cool cellar. Most of the boxes had come from behind the liquor store and, as she reached for the closest one, she read the label. *Tanqueray.* A smile curled on her lips as she thought of Hazel.

She flashed back to their scuffle in the water, and a chord of satisfaction thrummed through her blood. It was wondrous to have Hazel trapped between her thighs. The curve of Hazel's hips had pressed against the inside of her legs, and the way Hazel had twisted back and forth to free herself was still crystal clear.

Hazel's seeming reluctance to break contact was not lost on her. Having her in her arms had been just *right*. Andy flexed her fingers, recalling Hazel's biceps in her hands. She longed to have her hands on much more than that. Andy's thoughts had just begun to drift on other places for her digits when a shadow in the doorway caught her attention.

A black beast with horns blocked the sun streaming through the cellar door. Andy stumbled back and quickly gasped for air. The next second, the figure let out a soft bark. It was Anubis.

"Christ, boy!" She took a deep breath and looked at him. "You scared the shit out of me." She smiled and moved toward the entrance. Anubis took a step back, swung in a circle, and then stopped to look at her again. "What is it?" He stomped his feet impatiently. "Is something wrong?" *Hazel.* Cold washed over her.

Then she remembered that Nubi was *Paddy's* service dog. She nodded to Nubi. "Lead on." He seemed to understand because he took off at a trot down the slope of the yard and toward the road, checking over his shoulder to see that she was following. Andy, too, picked up her pace, afraid of what she would find.

When they reached Hazel's house, Andy began calling

for Paddy. Anubis led her to the small greenhouse, where she heard a muffled voice.

"In here!"

She entered the little building and blinked. The space was filled with some of the most vibrant colors Andy had ever seen in nature. Greens and pinks, purples and blues, yellows and oranges all rioting in a harnessed chaos of color.

"Mr. Quinn?"

"In the back. Got stuck."

Andy followed the voice and saw a pair of brown work boots extruding from beneath a table stacked with pots, soil, and sundry tools. "What's the best way to help?"

Paddy raised a hand from behind the table. "Just pull me on out, if you don't mind."

She stepped near to find that he was wedged between the wall and the table. Andy took hold of his hand, flexed her knees and leveraged Paddy up slowly and carefully. He grunted with the effort as she helped him prop against the table. Andy moved back far enough to give him space but remained close enough to catch him if necessary.

"Quite the tight spot."

"You're not kidding." He laughed shakily. "I dropped my glove behind the table and tried to retrieve it. Lost my balance." He regarded her with those eyes so much like his daughter's, his brows bent in question. "How did you know to come find me?"

Andy pointed to Anubis. "Hell of a dog you've got there, Mr. Quinn."

He smiled and put out a hand to the shepherd mix. "Good boy, Nubi."

The dog came and rubbed beneath the outstretched hand contentedly with a small whine.

"May I help you to the porch?"

"I would appreciate that."

Once they were settled into the rocking chairs, silence fell between them. Anubis trotted over and lay down with his head on his paws. Andy felt compelled to make conversation and so began asking Paddy what he knew about canned goods.

"I'm just not sure what to do with all of it."

"Well, I know Darcy used to share her extras with families around town."

"Did she?"

He rubbed his chin, and his face took on a thoughtful expression. "The church would probably have a list. I could get that information to you. Or you could just drop the food by there."

"The church?"

"Or if that doesn't suit you, Hazel could get it over there."

The idea of Hazel at church seemed disjointed, somehow. She had a hard time imagining Hazel in a pew singing "How Great Thou Art." Possibly Andy was projecting her own difficulties with religion, but she knew as well as anyone that church was hard to avoid in Alabama. In Birmingham, there were quite a few queer-affirming churches. Cooperative Baptists, Presbyterians, and Episcopalians were usually pretty open-minded, in Andy's experience. She seriously doubted that attitude extended this far out into the country.

"Hazel goes to church regularly?"

Paddy gave a small chuckle. "It depends on how you define *regularly*. She's always there Christmas and Easter and any time there's a wedding or funeral. Hazel doesn't particularly care for organized religion."

"And you?"

He looked at her as though trying to determine the reason

behind her interest. "I've been at church most of the Sundays in my life, but what you're really asking is if it bothers me that Hazel doesn't put the same value in it."

Andy smiled. "You're very sharp, Mr. Quinn."

"Paddy," he corrected. "It doesn't bother me. Hazel's spiritual practice is her own. She's a good person. She loves her neighbor, whoever they might be. Her heart is good and that's what matters. The rest of that stuff is for biblical scholars. I'm just a retired history teacher."

"I wish my parents had been of that opinion," Andy said. "They were rather the opposite of you. They were hung up on the appearance of goodness but were judgmental, self-righteous, and ungenerous." *I sound ungrateful.* "Not that they were *bad* people, just not as holy as they wanted everyone to think. When I came out—" She stopped abruptly. Andy was shocked at how easy it was to speak about her personal life with Paddy. Like Hazel, Paddy was genuine and truly seemed to listen when she spoke. After years at court, the experience was a novel one.

"Came out as gay?"

"Yes, that."

Andy took a breath, but Paddy didn't flinch. He just continued to rock back and forth in the rocking chair.

"My parents made me swear not to tell anyone. They were so concerned with how it would look to everyone else that they didn't consider the message they were sending me."

"That you weren't enough."

"Yes."

Paddy let out a sigh. "That's tough, Andy. I'm sorry."

She cleared her throat. "They had a lot of money. I think it was hard for them to accept it was something they couldn't throw money at and fix."

"And now?" Paddy asked after a few moments of rocking in silence. "Did they ever figure it out?"

"No, actually. Dad passed away a couple of years ago and I touch base with Mom every few weeks."

"It's too bad you didn't know Darcy." He smiled across the space between them. "She loved everyone just where they were at."

"The more I hear about her, the more I feel like I missed out." Again, Andy felt a sinking sensation just as she had that day on the creek. There was a part of her that felt Darcy would have seen her. *Really* seen her.

"Ask Hazel about her. Get her to share some of the hijinks they got up to. It might be good for both of you."

"Maybe." Andy's throat was raw with unexpressed emotion. "It was nice to sit with you, Paddy, but I really must get back to work."

"Of course, Sister." He smiled. "Thank you for rescuing me."

"I'm glad I was home. If you ever need me, just give me a call." Andy left him with her cell phone number and stepped lightly off the porch and back into the June heat. Her head buzzed.

She loved her parents. Had idolized her father. But the fact that they had chosen to prioritize their image over her had permanently damaged their relationship. She wondered what life would have been like with people like Darcy and Paddy surrounding her.

Then again, Hazel wasn't out in her community. Andy easily understood why. After all, living authentically and genuinely had cost her dearly. Andy had been willing to pay the price and would not go back to lying to herself or others, but she couldn't expect Hazel to have the same opinion.

Hazel's life was her own. Andy knew she should avoid getting romantically involved with Hazel.

If they had a relationship, it would be incredibly complicated. Andy couldn't ask Hazel to upend her life by coming out.

Andy couldn't hide her feelings.

And she couldn't stay away from Hazel Quinn.

Shit.

❖

That weekend, Hazel got home later than usual and found her father on her porch, quietly rocking back and forth. Nubi stood to greet her, his tail wagging with a soft swishing sound that made her smile. "Evening, Dad."

"Evening." He smiled at her, but he seemed far away.

"Been here long?"

He looked at his watch. "Just an hour or so."

Hazel couldn't put her finger on it, but something seemed slightly off. She sat heavily in the chair beside him and looked out across the lawn. "What are you thinking?"

After a moment's pause, he responded. "That I'm one lucky feller."

"Oh? How's that?"

"I've got a great family and a good community. I've never once felt like I didn't belong. Or that I wasn't good enough to do something."

Hazel wondered where this was coming from. It wasn't melancholy exactly, but it did seem like something had triggered this train of thought. "Did you watch some sort of human-interest story on TV today?"

He grinned, snapping out of his faraway stare. "No,

Wildflower. Sorry to scare you. I was just thinking about how some folks don't have what we have." He took her hand. "You know you can always count on me, don'tcha?"

An unexpected lump formed in Hazel's throat. "Yeah, Pops, I know."

"Good." He nodded and turned his gaze on some hummingbirds. They were very interested in the coral honeysuckle growing on the abandoned clothesline in the side\ yard. The little birds flitted about, chasing one another off then returning to drink greedily from the tubular blooms. "Now, tell me about your day. Anything interesting?"

"Not much." She stretched her legs, and her calves released their corded tension. "Oh. Actually, I did learn that our neighbor is snatching up property along Main Street. It looks like she's planning to renovate some lots to sell."

"Well, that's good, right?"

"Yeah, I just worry she'll alter the face of the town too much."

"Don't we have a historical society?"

"Yes." Hazel sighed. "But the rules and regulations for what can and can't be done are pretty vague." She had researched Green Valley Historical Society's guidelines for remodeling buildings in designated historic districts, and none of it was specific enough, in her opinion. "I just have concerns."

"Why don't you just talk to her about it?" Paddy said this like it was the most logical thing in the world.

"Just call her up and say what? 'Hey, don't screw up my town'?" She shook her head. "No. And I don't have her number anyway."

"I have her number right here."

Hazel was surprised. "When did that happen?"

Paddy suddenly wouldn't meet her eye. "A few days ago."

Hazel was suspicious. "And she just, what? Walked over here and gave you her number?"

"No." He sighed and turned to meet her gaze. "A few days ago, I fell in the greenhouse. I wasn't hurt, but Nubi went to get Andy. She helped me to the porch and stayed with me awhile."

"I've seen her twice in as many days! Why didn't she mention this to me? Why didn't you, for that matter?" Hazel bubbled with hot anger. It was really fear, but that didn't stop her from scolding her father. "After the last time—"

"I didn't want to worry you." He paused. "As for Andy, I can't speak for her motives."

"Give me her number and I'll ask her myself."

Paddy shook his head. "I'm not going to aid you in harassing that woman."

"Fine." Hazel stood abruptly. She was frustrated and more than a little concerned by the news of her father's tumble. "I'll just walk over there."

She marched down the steps and across the street to Andy's house. She had already knocked on the door before she had second thoughts. *I really don't have much of a leg to stand on.* Both her father and Andy were their own people and couldn't be forced to disclose information they didn't want to share. But the idea of Paddy helpless on the ground caused more anger to bubble to the surface. When the door finally opened, Hazel barely gave Andy a chance to speak.

"Hazel? Is everything—?"

"Did you help my father after a fall and not tell me about it?"

The open expression on Andy's face suddenly disappeared, and in its place was the familiar aspect of cool professionalism. "Would you like to come in?"

"No, I would like an answer."

Andy seemed unmoved by the vehemence in Hazel's voice. They stood staring at one another for a moment.

"Please, come in." Andy repeated the invitation.

Hazel nodded jerkily and walked across the threshold. Before she took three steps into the high-ceilinged foyer, however, she rounded on Andy again. "Please answer my question."

Andy tucked her hands into her pockets. She looked so cool and confident that Hazel wanted to shake her. From her trim, peach button down to her stone-gray trousers, Andy was the picture of sophistication and stoicism.

"I was working in the cellar when Anubis came to visit," she began in a calm tone. "I realized something must be wrong and so I followed him home. I found your father in the greenhouse. He was stuck but unharmed. I checked him when I pulled him out and then sat with him for a while afterward to make sure he didn't have any injuries."

"How did you know to follow Anubis?" Hazel was sidetracked from her original question.

"He's a service dog. I read somewhere you're supposed to follow them if they show up without their owner." Andy shifted her stance. "Hazel, if Paddy had been injured, I would have called you immediately. He didn't have a scratch on him. No bruises, no swelling, nothing. I checked. He was perfectly lucid while we held a conversation." Something flickered in her eyes and her face softened, but it was gone before Hazel could analyze the change.

"Why didn't you tell me when you saw me this week?" Hazel made an effort to soften her tone, though she was still angry.

"I assumed Paddy would tell you when he was ready."

"And if he never did?"

"Then neither would I."

"Even knowing I would be furious?"

Andy smiled and took a step forward, bringing them closer together. "Yes, even knowing that."

Hazel was exasperated. "But why? I have a right to know."

"Paddy has a right to his dignity. I can't imagine what it's like to have your body betray you like that. To have trouble with something as simple as retrieving a fallen glove. To require rescue from someone you barely know." She shook her head. "I'm sorry you're upset, but I would do it the exact same way again because I respect your father's right to privacy."

Hazel didn't know what to say. How could she express what it meant to her that Andy was so concerned for her father's dignity? Failing to find words, she took a step forward, grasped Andy's collar, and pulled Andy's lips to her own. They were softened by surprise but soon took form and returned Hazel's kiss. Andy nipped gently at her bottom lip and Hazel let her in automatically.

Andy's tongue was smooth and strong and purposeful. Hazel let Andy seduce her mouth as Hazel's grip on Andy's collar tightened. Arms encircled her waist and pulled her closer as Andy continued to suck, flick, and nip until Hazel was trembling. With a monumental effort, Hazel broke the kiss and pushed away.

"I—I'm sorry." She tried to slow her breathing and her hammering heart. "I shouldn't have just grabbed you like that. I have to go."

Andy stepped back as if to allow her plenty of space. "Good night, Hazel," she said calmly.

Hazel didn't respond but opened the door and went out onto the porch. The coolness of night enveloped her. She almost expected to see steam rise from her skin in the dewy air. God, what had she done? Just thrown herself at Andy Richter?

She could still feel Andy's tongue and taste the bourbon on her lips. And Andy had just taken it in stride as though she'd been expecting it. As though she'd been waiting for it.

No. Hazel shook her head. That wasn't true. Andy had been surprised, at least at first. Hazel imagined her face had held pure shock the way it had when she'd dunked Andy in the lake. It hadn't taken her long, though, to take control of the situation. Just as she had at the lake. Arousal shivered up her back. Andy was always so *poised*. As though rarely caught off-guard. Hazel was proud to have surprised her twice.

She just had to figure out what the hell she was going to do now.

CHAPTER EIGHT

The next week found Hazel collecting rent. She both loved and hated this task. Handling money was her least favorite thing to do, but the opportunity to speak with everyone and get the news around town fed her soul. She loved her community and enjoyed nothing better than being in it.

As she stepped out of the pharmacy, a voice called her name. Hazel turned to see Raine waving her down. Smiling, she made her way to where Raine stood, leaning against her mid-80s blue Chevy truck. Her red heeler was in the back of the truck and watched Hazel closely as she approached, sniffing the air vigorously.

"Hey, Sunny." Hazel spoke to the dog as she got closer. Sunny's stumpy tail wagged the tiniest amount. "Hey, you." She smiled at Raine.

"Hey." Raine's smile was soft.

Hazel ignored the affection in Raine's green eyes. "How are things?"

"Good, just trying to keep cool. The horses have been listless in this weather." Raine launched into the precautions she'd taken to ensure the safety of her herd. Hazel feigned interest. "But enough about that," Raine said finally. "How are you? I see you're busy making big renovations downtown."

Hazel frowned. "Me? I don't think so."

Raine knit her brows together. "Don't you own those storefronts on the south side of Main Street?"

"No, I'm on the other side. I think Andy Richter just bought all that."

"Andy." Raine said the name flatly. "The snob from the auction."

Hazel bristled but remained friendly. "She can come across like that, but she's actually a nice person."

"Hmm," Raine said in a dubious tone. "Well, she's got a whole bunch of equipment over there at those stores like she's going to rip them apart."

"Surely not." Hazel frowned and shook her head.

Raine put her hands in the air. "Look, all I'm saying is that it doesn't look like a simple paint job. Might should put in a call to the historical society, but I doubt they could do anything about it. She was a lawyer, wasn't she? I bet she knows all the loopholes."

Hazel didn't want to believe this. She knew Andy had integrity…

She also knew Andy wanted to make money like every other business owner. Hazel didn't like the idea of her modernizing the entire street.

"I'll drive over there and have a look."

"Better you than me," Raine called behind her.

❖

Hazel parked at the curb and exited her vehicle in a hurry. She approached the sidewalk and surveyed the equipment. It sure did look like Andy was up to some heavy renovations, beginning with taking out walls. She stepped closer to peer into one of the storefronts to see that some of the brick walls had been disassembled.

"Damn it." She hadn't wanted to believe it, but here was the evidence in front of her face. "We'll see about this," she murmured. She marched across the square to Andy's office, yanked open the door and walked into the cool building. Hazel then blinked in the dimness.

She could hear Andy's voice through the closed back room door and assumed Andy was on a call with someone. She thought about taking a chair in the waiting room but was too uptight to sit. Instead, she wandered the waiting area, looking at the tasteful artwork on the walls and grudgingly admiring the way the colors of the walls and floorboards complemented one another.

She heard Andy end the call, and a few seconds later, she opened the door and looked out. When she saw Hazel, she smiled.

"Can we talk?" Hazel asked abruptly.

Andy's brow furrowed, but she stepped back to allow Hazel into the office and then turned to shut the door. "What am I in trouble for this time?"

Hazel didn't like the mocking tone she heard in Andy's voice. "You're tearing apart those buildings on the square." She didn't even try to keep the accusation out of her voice.

Andy crossed her arms over her chest. "I am doing no such thing."

"I drove over there after Raine—"

"Raine Lewis?" Andy frowned. "She's the one who gave you this information?"

"Yes." Hazel raised her chin. "I was collecting rent when I saw her at the pharmacy."

"I'm sure she was eager to share her gossip."

"She told me you had a lot of equipment at those properties on Main. I didn't want to believe that you would tear down those historical buildings, but I saw what I saw."

"What *did* you see?" Andy asked quietly.

"Dust and bricks all over the place. The storefronts opened to the street. A mess."

"A mess is what you have to make when you rebuild, Hazel."

The smallest amount of doubt flickered in Hazel's mind. "Rebuild?"

"Yes. The roof was compromised and has been leaking for years. There's damage beyond repair. I hired an extensive crew to rebuild the stores according to the original layouts. The bricks you saw were the originals that I'm replacing with new ones inside. I'll use the old ones on the storefronts so that they look like they did before. I checked with Green Valley Historical Society, and they approved all of this."

"Oh." Hazel deflated and trained her eyes to a spot on the wall just past Andy's left ear. "I see."

"Do you have so little faith in me?"

The softness of her tone snapped Hazel's eyes back to Andy's face.

"I'm sorry," she said quietly. "I knew better, really, I just got caught up in the moment."

Andy smiled and Hazel knew she'd been forgiven.

"You seem to do that a good bit. Get caught up in the moment."

"Do I?"

"Dunking me"—Andy ticked off on her long fingers—"charging over to my house last week and accosting me here."

"It does sound bad when you list it off like that...I'm a bit impulsive."

"I think you lack discipline."

Hazel arched a brow. "Oh? And I suppose you know how to fix that?"

"Sure." Andy arched a brow in return. "Lean over the desk."

The room went silent as Hazel's heart skipped a bit. Her stomach was suddenly somersaulting, and something a whole lot like arousal skittered up her spine. "Excuse me?"

Andy stepped close with one smooth, predatory step. Hazel was rooted to the spot. She couldn't have retreated even if she wanted. And she definitely wanted to?

"Lean over the desk," Andy repeated.

"I think you've misunderstood something."

"No, I don't think I have. I intend to spank you."

Hazel didn't know what to do. She wanted Andy's hands on her desperately. Andy was more than capable of pleasing her; falling into her bed was bound to be an incredibly erotic experience. A part of her relished the idea of handing over control to such a capable woman. But a *spanking*? She couldn't wrap her head around it.

"I—I can't!" Hazel was unsure how to describe her feelings. The way Andy looked at her drove everything but desire from her mind. How often had she fantasized about Andy's strong arms and capable hands?

"You could. You could if you wanted to." Andy stepped a little closer. "I think you want to." Hazel allowed Andy to take her hand, bring it to her lips and press a soft kiss to her skin.

"I do want to. I just…" She took a deep breath and looked into Andy's blue, blue eyes.

"I'm an experienced lover and I wouldn't harm you." Andy spoke softly as she positioned herself so that their thighs were grazing. One of her firm, strong hands stroked between Hazel's shoulder blades and down to press confidently at the small of her back. "I will only spank your backside. The safe word is *red*, if you consent."

There was a trail of fire where Andy's hand caressed her. She wanted this very badly. "I consent," Hazel said quickly as heat rose in her face and her pulse throbbed between her legs. "I've never done anything like this." She swallowed forcibly against her suddenly dry mouth. "*Red* is the safe word?"

"Yes. If you get scared or want to stop, just say *red* and I will stop immediately." Andy met her gaze. "Are you sure you want to try it?"

"Yes," Hazel said. "Yes, I would."

Andy guided her with firm but gentle hands to the desk and pressed her to it. The desk was solid against the top of her thighs, and Hazel couldn't bring herself to lean over its surface, though a shiver of anticipation snaked up her spine.

"Bend," Andy said softly and encouraged Hazel with a hand on her lower back once more.

Hazel did as she was told and pressed her right cheek to the oak desktop. Her legs were trembling slightly, and her breathing was rapid, but she was wet. Undeniably wet. Andy lifted her prairie skirt just enough to reach beneath. "I—"

"I think six licks should do it."

"Six?" Hazel was expecting less. Andy had pulled that number out of nowhere.

"Yes, six. You've charged me three times. That's two swats per altercation. Sounds fair to me...Shall we begin?"

"Yes." Hazel immediately tensed, preparing for a spank, but rather than Andy coming down on her backside, she ran her hand teasingly up the back of Hazel's right thigh and plucked at her underwear. Hazel shuddered and bit down on her tongue to fight back a moan. Andy hadn't really begun, but the anticipation was killing Hazel.

"What color is your underwear, Hazel?"

Hazel could barely think but mustered a reply. "Why don't you just look?"

Andy gave her a gentle rap on her right buttock and then smoothed her hand down its curve. "That's one. I asked you a question."

Hazel was dizzy with desire. Or maybe she was dizzy because she'd forgotten to breathe. "Pink."

"Mmm." Andy hummed approvingly and molded the flesh of Hazel's backside with one hand. "Are they silk?"

Before Hazel could answer, however, the sound of the outside door met her ears. Andy stepped back, dropped her skirt, and pulled her upright. The quick motions momentarily disoriented Hazel, who looked about in a daze.

"What—?"

"Just when you're about to eat," Andy grumbled. She went to the door of the office, opened it, and stepped out.

Hazel could hear her greeting someone, maybe a potential client. She needed to leave but couldn't get her legs to cooperate. With a great effort, she composed herself and nodded to the man as he came around the corner behind Andy.

"Oh, I see you're busy."

"Not at all," Andy replied casually. "Hazel and I are neighbors and can conclude our business later." Andy looked at Hazel. "Right, Ms. Quinn?"

"Right." Hazel smiled at the man and then turned her attention to Andy. "I'll catch you another time, then."

"Any evening." Andy smirked. "You know where to find me."

❖

By the end of the week, Hazel was congratulating herself on avoiding Andy. She'd seen her from a distance a few times, but each time she'd been able to turn around or pretend not to notice. She simply could not face her after what had transpired in Andy's office at the beginning of the week.

The memory of leaning over, her face pressed to the cool wooden surface of the desk, still made her hot. The experience had simultaneously been too much and not enough. Andy's gentle hands caressing up her leg and over the curve of her ass had lit her on fire. Just recalling the anticipation of Andy striking her accelerated her heartbeat. Waiting. Wondering how much strength Andy would use and how badly it would sting.

The experience had certainly been illuminating. She'd never relinquished control like that. Ever. But even with her backside in the air, Hazel had felt safe. Not for a second had she been afraid. Even now, she regretted they had been interrupted.

At the same time that Hazel longed for Andy's solid heat behind her once more, this desire concerned her. It was all she could think about. Hazel couldn't get Andy out of her head. She was distracted, and it was interfering with her work. There were a multitude of people who depended on her. Green Valley had always come first, and this infatuation with Andy Ritcher was creating friction where there had never been any.

Hazel wasn't looking to complicate anything. She liked the way her life was and didn't want to turn it upside down. Her rule for dating exclusively out of town was in place for a reason. Coming out to her community just wasn't on her agenda. No matter how badly she wanted Andy.

But what if?

Hazel momentarily entertained the idea of waking next to Andy, meeting her for lunch dates, and preparing for cozy holiday seasons with her. She imagined sharing the burdens of her work and shouldering Andy's. Her stomach fluttered with butterflies. It was an alluring dream. But she just couldn't.

She shook her head to dislodge domestic images of cooking with Andy, gardening with Andy, kneeling between Andy's legs and—

Hazel pulled herself to reality's surface with a tremendous and abrupt wrench. No, she *lusted* after Andy. That was all. It was a simple matter of willpower. And Hazel had willpower in spades.

Guiding her car down the drive of her home, she found her father in his usual place on the porch with Nubi at his feet. Hazel grabbed her bag, got out, and made her way up the steps, still trying to shake her desires away.

"Hey, Pops."

"Hey, Wildflower." He smiled. "How was your day?"

"Pretty good." She took the seat beside him.

"You won't mind that I volunteered you for something, then, will you?"

Hazel smiled. "Of course not. What am I up to this time?"

"Well, you know Darcy put up tons of canned goods every year?"

"Yup, always had a cellar full, as I recall."

"Well, Andy has gone through all of it and doesn't want to throw it away." Hazel's blood tingled at the mention of Andy's name. "I told her Darcy used to donate it to families in the community."

"I recall that."

"So, I volunteered you to help her load all that up and get it to the church."

"Oh, yeah, I can do that." She couldn't avoid Andy forever.

"Figured it would be difficult for her to get all those boxes in her little coupe."

"Probably." Hazel smiled.

"I like her."

Hazel turned to look at Paddy. She was surprised by his straightforward admission. "You do, huh?"

"And not just because she pulled me outta that tight spot." He chuckled. "She comes across like a tough guy, but she's got a soft heart. Which is saying something after what she's been through."

Not for the first time, Hazel wondered just exactly what Andy and her father had discussed that day on the porch after Paddy's rescue. "Got her figured out, huh?"

Her father shook his head with a smile. "I don't know about all that, but I'm glad you two are friends." Paddy met her eyes briefly and intensely. "Now, get going."

"What?" Hazel was surprised. "You want me to load that stuff tonight?"

"It's better not to put things off, Hazel. You know this."

"I…" Hazel *did* know it. "Alright, I won't argue."

"That's a first."

"Hey!" She laughed. "Will you want dinner when I get back?"

"Nah, I'm not waiting up. Andy said there were *a lot* of boxes."

"Well, I'll get changed and head on over, then."

"You gals have fun!"

Hazel hoped she had successfully wiped all emotion from her face.

CHAPTER NINE

A ndy had just sat down at her office desk when she heard a knock on the door. At first, she wanted to ignore it. She had a great deal to do and hadn't even unpacked her briefcase yet. Curiosity got the better of her, however. She rose from her chair and passed through the house to the foyer.

She recognized Hazel's shape through the diamond-patterned panes of glass in the window panels. A smile curved over her features. Andy wondered what had brought Hazel to her steps when she'd tried so hard to avoid Andy all week. Regardless of the cause, Andy wasn't going to squander the chance to finish what she had started.

Hazel knocked again and Andy opened the door. "Good evening."

"Good evening. Dad sent me over to help with the canned goods." Hazel spoke quickly as though trying to set the tone for the encounter.

"Ah, wonderful. I'll just get the key to the cellar. You can follow me through the back, if you like."

"Uh, sure."

Andy turned and strode through the foyer to the kitchen. Hazel trailed several steps behind. *I suppose she thinks she's safe*. The key was hanging on a rack by the back door. Andy took the key, opened the back kitchen door, then gestured Hazel through with a small bow. Hazel stepped lightly down the new steps and turned to look at Andy as she followed.

"Those steps are new."

"Yes, that was one of the first things I took care of when I moved in. Those boards were rotten. It's a wonder Aunt Darcy didn't go right through them."

"The last few years or so, she rarely went out the back. She mostly used the front door. She didn't even have a car."

"She didn't?"

Hazel smiled. "No. She would walk over to my house and borrow Dad's truck sometimes. He always leaves the keys in the ignition."

"Was she averse to driving?"

"Well, for the longest time she had a mule that she took everywhere."

Andy was surprised. "What about during the winter? Did it have an enclosed cab?"

They had reached the cellar door when Hazel stopped and blinked. "A cab? Of course not. She would just bundle up."

Andy thought this comment was odd. Not to mention Hazel's tone. Something slid into place. "Wait, are we talking about an actual mule? Like donkey and horse mule?"

"Yes, that's what I said."

"I thought you were talking about the utility vehicle!" Andy was incredulous. "My great-aunt rode an actual mule to town?"

"Yes, well up into her seventies. Until Horace died. He's buried out back in the pine forest."

"There's a portrait of a mule in the office. I never considered that she actually rode the animal."

Hazel smiled and seemed to relax for the first time since

seeing Andy. "I'll bring some photographic evidence over soon." She turned to the cellar. "Now, the boxes. Dad said you have a lot of them."

Andy opened the wooden doors, careful not to let them slam. "Well, I thought I would, but I decided to keep more of the canned goods than I expected. I only ended up with nine boxes to donate."

"That's plenty enough, though."

Andy stepped down and raised the first box. "They're pretty heavy." She held it up to Hazel, who took it without hesitation.

"I think I can manage." She turned and started around the side of the house toward her car. Andy grabbed the next box with a grin.

By the time they had all nine boxes loaded into Hazel's Subaru, they were sweating. The sun had sunk beneath the tree line, but the grass and earth were still radiating the heat of the day.

"What I wouldn't give for a glass of your lemonade." Andy pushed back her hair.

"I would invite you over, but I'm fresh out."

"How about a glass of cold lemon water? I made some mint ice cubes yesterday."

"Really?" Hazel turned to look at her.

"I'm not completely useless in a kitchen." Andy laughed. "On hot days, I like to put a splash of lemon water in my bourbon." She turned to lead Hazel back into the house. "Would you like to try it?"

"Yes, please." Hazel followed her into the kitchen.

Andy took a shallow pan from the freezer and used tongs to put several ice cubes in tumblers. She poured a shot of bourbon in each and then splashed lemon water over the liquor. After swirling one glass, she offered it to Hazel.

"Mmm," Hazel said after swirling it herself and taking a slow sip. "Very nice."

"I'm glad you like it."

Andy took a sip of her drink and then put away all the ingredients before turning back to Hazel. She snapped her fingers. "Oh! I forgot! I'd like to show you something." Andy turned and motioned for Hazel to follow. "In the study."

"Study?" Hazel frowned but followed after another sip of her drink.

"The room Darcy used as an art studio; I turned it into a study. It's the only room I'm even close to finishing." She led her into the room and put her drink down on the coffee table. "I framed a few canvases I found and hung them up."

Hazel came to the room and stopped in the doorway. Andy watched as she also moved to put her drink down on the table and then approached the first piece of artwork on the wall. Hazel ran her hand over the lines and ridges in the landscape.

"This is the view from Monte Sano," Hazel said softly before moving to the next picture. "And this is the spring behind the house." She got to the next picture and laughed. "This is Horace. God, she did a great job on this one. That was his expression exactly!"

Andy slowly traced Hazel's steps as she traveled along the wall toward the ornate antique desk. Her skirt stirred as she walked. Andy was certain Hazel had been wearing cuffed overalls earlier in the day when she had seen her exiting the town's post office. So, she had changed before coming over to load canned goods. *I think I know what this means.* Hazel turned back to her, and Andy wrenched herself back to the conversation.

"There were other canvases. I stored them in the attic, but you could take a look sometime if you would like."

"Was this what you wanted to show me?"

"No, actually." Andy took a step forward, and Hazel shifted back. She smiled as Hazel's eyes flickered around the room. *There's no graceful escape, Hazel.* "It was the desk."

"The desk?" Hazel repeated faintly and looked over her shoulder at the luxurious piece of furniture.

"I got it at an antique dealer last week. I've had my eye on it for some time." Andy moved closer still while speaking. "I thought it fit the style of the room."

"Oh, yes. I agree." Hazel seemed reluctant to turn to look at the desk.

"Would you like a closer look?"

"A c-closer look?" Hazel's voice broke.

Andy closed the gap between them and traced Hazel's jaw gently. Hazel's eyes were wide, but she melted against Andy as she pressed between her legs. "I was disappointed when we were interrupted the other day. I was looking forward to disciplining you." She moved her fingers over Hazel's soft mouth. Her eyes were no longer round, but inquisitive and glittering. "Would you like to continue?"

"I want that." Hazel rolled her body against Andy's with a motion that sent waves of heat rioting through her blood.

"You consent?"

"Yes!"

"Turn around." Andy kept her voice soft, but firm. "Remember, if you want to stop, you say *red*."

"Yes, I know."

Andy smiled at the eagerness in Hazel's voice. "Six licks, was it?" She caressed Hazel through her skirt.

"Five," Hazel corrected her. "You s-spanked me once before we stopped."

"Five?" Andy teased. "Are you sure?" She abruptly jerked Hazel's skirt to the floor. It puddled at her ankles.

Hazel gasped and then shuddered when Andy filled her hands with Hazel's backside reverently. "I'm sure."

"Very well, then." Andy casually plucked at the French-cut underwear. "Mmm, black lace. You shouldn't have."

"I didn't wear it for *you*."

Smack. The swipe wasn't gentle, but neither was it harsh. The flesh of Hazel's backside reddened anyway. "One," Andy said quietly. "Does your bra match?" Hazel didn't respond. Andy bent Hazel at the waist until she was pressed against the dark wood of the desk and then spanked her again with the same force. "Two, I asked a question." Her voice was calm, but Hazel trembled from head to toe.

"Yes!" She growled. "It's a matching set."

"And you wore it for me."

"No—"

Andy struck her again. Somewhat harder. Hard enough she knew the strike stung. Hazel groaned. "Three," Andy said softly as she caressed the reddened skin of Hazel's right buttock. "There's no need to lie, Hazel."

With her left hand, Andy began at the top of Hazel's black panties and ran her thumb down between her cheeks and into the valley of her folds. Hazel squirmed.

"I don't know what you want me to say." Hazel panted as Andy repeated the caress while squeezing her flesh with her other hand.

"I want you to tell the truth." Andy applied more pressure with her thumb so that she could just make out the erect pearl of Hazel's clitoris through the delicate underwear. "You want this."

"Yes, I want this, damn you!" Hazel burst. "I'm on fucking fire! Is that what you want to hear?"

Thwack! The delicious sound reverberated around the

room. "Four." Andy applied more pressure with her left hand and made tight circles around the hard bud between Hazel's legs. Hazel jerked and then moaned loudly. "That is exactly what I wanted to hear. You have one more swat left. Would you like for it to be hard or soft?"

"Oh, God, Andy. That's…" Hazel sputtered. "I don't know!"

"You do know." Andy opened her palm and reached into Hazel's panties to rub her soaking sex with quick precision. "Hard or soft?"

"Hard!"

Andy smirked and spanked her hard. She then drove Hazel over the edge with her other hand. Hazel cried out and thrust against Andy's palm rhythmically until she collapsed bonelessly against the gleaming rosewood desk.

Slowly, Andy stepped back from Hazel and gently turned her around. She took Hazel's jaw in her hand and brought their lips together.

After a slow, exploring kiss, Hazel caught her breath and reached for Andy. "I want to touch you."

"I know." Andy reversed their positions so that she could lean back and prop her backside on the desk. She stripped down her trousers and underwear, hoping Hazel didn't notice the shake in her hands. Andy put a hand on Hazel's shoulder and urged her to her knees. "Touch me, please," she said softly.

Hazel groaned and nuzzled forward into the dark blond pelt between Andy's thighs. One flick of her tongue and Andy's knuckles whitened on the edge of the desk. She clutched the polished wood hard enough that the sharp corner bit into her palms. It was all she could do to stay quiet as Hazel's tongue laved back and forth, spreading her lips over and over. Andy fought for control. She looked down and realized too late that this was a mistake. The tops of Hazel's round breasts were visible in the dip of her blouse. They strained against the black lace bra. Andy's mouth watered.

When Hazel took her clitoris behind her lips and sucked hard, Andy's hips jerked of their own accord. Hazel grasped her thighs tightly and pushed them farther apart. Andy placed a hand on the back of Hazel's head and urged her forward.

"Finish me." Her voice was strained, but the command was there all the same.

Hazel did as she was bid while Andy hung on to the desk like it was her lifeline in a raging sea. She arched and threw her head back with a groan as she came hard against Hazel's mouth. The spasms racked her body hard. When Hazel rose to her feet, Andy pulled her close and claimed her mouth. She could taste her musk on Hazel's lips.

Hazel pulled back. "That was…" She trailed off, seemingly unable to put words to the experience.

"Vigorous?" Andy supplied. "Amazing?"

"Hot."

Andy laughed and stood as Hazel retrieved her skirt. The trousers on the floor were wrinkled, but Andy put them on, nonetheless. She didn't have much of a choice.

"Worth the wait?"

"I'm not going to answer that at the risk of stroking your already enormous ego."

Andy laughed but was not offended. "You were surprised you enjoyed that."

Hazel blushed. Andy loved the color.

"I meant it when I said that I'd never done that. Had that done to me."

"But you enjoyed it." Hazel nodded and looked away. Andy grabbed her face and planted a firm kiss on her lips. "There's no room for shame here."

"I'm not ashamed."

"Embarrassed?"

"Maybe."

"Why?" Andy crossed the room to put some space between them. She didn't want Hazel to feel pressured.

"I don't know. Surrendering is just not in my nature."

"Which is why you enjoyed it so immensely."

Hazel looked at her with a slight frown. "Hmm."

"Look, that sort of play isn't necessarily about the spanking itself. It's about handing over control to someone else. Someone you trust won't abuse that control. Surrendering in a safe way."

Hazel looked thoughtful. "Have you done that a lot?"

"Spanked my partners?" Andy grinned. "Not that often, actually. You're a special case."

"I'm honored." Hazel rolled her eyes.

Andy closed the distance once again but stayed just outside arm's length. "For the record, I don't typically come undone so quickly. What you did to me was spectacular."

"Really?" Hazel stepped closer and tentatively reached for her. "So, what now?"

Andy frowned. She didn't know what Hazel was asking. "What do you mean?"

"I mean, I don't typically fuck my neighbors and then drive home."

Hazel's tone of voice stung Andy. It was a shade too callous. She dropped her hands and eased back. "Neither do I, Hazel."

"I just meant," Hazel began in a softer tone as though she'd sensed the shift in Andy, "that this is uncharted territory for me."

"I don't have any expectations," Andy said truthfully. "I enjoy your company, and I enjoyed making love to you, but I know and understand your trepidation about taking a lover in your community. I respect that."

Hazel took a deep breath. "Okay," she responded. "That works for me."

"Good." Andy closed the gap once more to plant a chaste kiss on her lips. "You should probably head out before Paddy gets suspicious."

"Right."

Andy escorted her to the door and closed it behind her. She then turned and pressed her back to the solid surface. With a sigh, she dropped her head back and looked at the modest chandelier in the foyer.

What she said had been true. She really had no expectations. That didn't mean she didn't have hopes. *Stupid.* Hazel had been up front about not wanting a local relationship, and Andy had pursued her anyway, knowing damn well it could lead to conflict. In her defense, she'd not counted on *enjoying* Hazel as much as she did. More than enjoyed her…Andy cared for Hazel. It wasn't this revelation that shocked her, it was the fact she didn't mind admitting it.

She pushed from the door and went back to her office. She would just have to follow Hazel's lead in this. It was against her nature to *follow*, but she wouldn't push Hazel into a decision. She respected her too much. The idea of having to hide her affection and feelings for Hazel was abhorrent, but it was the position she'd put herself in and she'd just have to deal with it.

CHAPTER TEN

A s Hazel sat with her coffee on the porch the next morning, she contemplated the day ahead. She'd received a call from the manager at the Corner Stop and Shop about a leaking pipe. She knew the preparation and repair would take most of the day and require a trip to the hardware store. Hazel dreaded and relished these sorts of projects. They were a lot of work, and labor in July was unbearable in Alabama. On the other hand, she always felt very accomplished after the completion of these tasks.

As she considered accelerating her biannual check of the utilities and structural soundness of all the Quinn properties, Hazel watched Andy's coupe pull out from the magnolia-flanked drive and onto the rough road. Andy carefully picked her way around potholes until she was out of sight. Hazel assumed she was headed to her office.

Despite what Andy had said about having no expectations about their relationship, Hazel mused over her position on it. The sex was undeniably hot. No, more than that. It was the best she'd ever had. She had no problem admitting it. The sex was amazing, in part, because she had come to *know* Andy.

She could also admit she wanted to know Andy more through intimacy. She was eager to see what else Andy was capable of. She just didn't want other people to know about it.

Hazel wasn't quite sure where that left them. As much as Hazel hated labels, she felt the need to name this nebulous thing between them. *Are we friends with benefits?* She'd had a couple of arrangements like that before, but this didn't feel the same. Hazel watched a caterpillar squiggle its way down the porch rail like a thick, dirty pipe cleaner. She leaned forward to get a better look, certain not to touch the creature. The long black filaments in the front and back looked like eyelashes. The slow, undulating motion of its body mesmerized her. Pulling herself from the reverie, she finished her coffee, stood, and began getting ready for work.

❖

Hazel pushed her thick braid back over her shoulder from where it was caught in the clasp of her cotton overalls. She was sweating. A lot. The leak began in a small utility closet with no fan or air flow. As soon as she walked in, Hazel realized she was going to need to replace the pipe and determine a way to keep the small closet dry. *Maybe a small dehumidifier with a drainage pipe into the floor sink?* She scribbled some notes on a flip-pad and tucked it into her pocket as she shouldered her small tool bag and exited the closet.

She grabbed a chilled lime-flavored sports drink and a protein bar on her way to the counter. Hazel shifted back and forth on the balls of her feet while she waited in line. The men in front of her were talking excitedly about a vehicle outside. She glanced out the glass doors to see a massive work truck rumbling loudly at the single, diesel pump.

"It's gotta be the new 3500," said the taller of the men.

"GMC?" the other man asked, craning around the spinning rack of sunglasses blocking his view.

"Naw, look at the dump-bed. It's definitely a Chevy."

"That is a serious work truck. No small-timer could afford that thing."

Hazel had not been incredibly interested up until this point. She also scrutinized the vehicle. The printing on the side of the truck said *Babcock Construction*. It sounded vaguely familiar, but not because she'd worked with them before. The men were right; this was a serious work truck. It wasn't the sort of thing a local would drive around for home repair or to build a barn. *Perhaps the driver is lost or just passing through.*

"Hazel?" The manager behind the counter called her name.

She blinked. The two men were gone, and she had been standing dreamily as she stared out of the window. With a laugh, she stepped forward.

"Sorry, Rich, was lost in thought."

"That bad, huh?" He gestured to the utility room.

"Oh, not at all." Hazel put down her purchases.

"You know I wouldn't charge you for your own merchandise."

Hazel frowned. "We've talked about this before. You charge everybody so that inventory is accurate. Even me."

"And Paddy?" The man grinned, knowing her tenderness for her father.

She laughed. "You charge *me* for whatever Dad buys, but someone pays nonetheless."

He threw up his hands, "I know, I know. You're such a serious businesswoman." Rich rang up the snacks and Hazel passed him a ten-dollar bill. He counted out her change and passed it back.

"That big truck out there, have they come through before?"

"Them? Oh, yeah, they came through here a couple of days ago."

"Really?"

"Yeah, haven't heard what they're working on, though."

"Hmm." Hazel put the change in her pocket. "Well, I'll be back in a couple of hours or so, Rich. The pipe will be fixed today."

"Thanks, Hazel."

"Don't thank me until it's done." She laughed. "A million things could go wrong."

❖

Hazel stepped into the hardware store with her notebook of measurements and stopped at the counter. It was a long counter and open on the other end. On the open side, there were a couple of lawn chairs where several older men and an older woman sat. At the tinkle of the bell, everyone turned to the door, but seeing that it was Hazel, no one stood. Amos threw up one hand in greeting and she made her way to the circle of old-timers.

"Hey there, Sister." Her uncle greeted her. Hazel kissed him on the cheek and smiled around at the others.

"Morning, y'all. Been a while, Frankie." She addressed the lanky old woman with long gray hair and sparkling green eyes.

"Yes, it has." The woman looked her up and down. "It was time for my monthly run to town."

Hazel always had the feeling that this woman, much like Darcy, could see through her. "I'm honored to see you, then." Hazel winked.

Frankie didn't return the grin, but her mouth twitched.

"We haven't talked since Darcy's funeral." She spoke in the blunt manner in which she did everything. It was her way.

"Sounds about right."

"You know this young Tom who's inherited Darcy's estate?"

It took Hazel a moment to realize Frankie was speaking about Andy. She looked for a reaction from her uncle and the others, but there was none. "Yeah, Andy Richter."

"Raine's got some opinions about her," Cliff piped in with a grin. "But I like her alright. Very down to earth, even if she's a little hard to read."

"Yeah, Andy's good people." Amos nodded and then turned back to his niece. "You need something?"

"Oh, yeah." She explained the supplies she needed and headed farther into the store with Amos.

Later, as Hazel loaded her purchases into the back of her father's truck, she heard her name. Frankie had followed her out of the store.

"Glad I caught you."

Hazel closed the tailgate and came around the pale-yellow hood of the truck. "Oh, yeah?" She dusted her hands and waved away the home-rolled cigarette Frankie offered.

"My brother wasn't joking when he said Raine had opinions about this Richter woman."

"I'm sure." Hazel fought not to roll her eyes. "Raine seems determined not to like her."

Frankie made a wry face and blew smoke through her nostrils. "You and I both know it's because Raine is crazy about you, and the new woman has your attention."

Hazel's mouth dropped open for a second, but she recovered enough to fight through the blush she felt rising on her cheeks. "I didn't think I'd been that obvious."

"You haven't been. But you're not the first lady-loving woman in this community, girl." Frankie waved as a passing truck honked. "I'm not in town much, but it doesn't mean I don't see what's going on."

The casual way Frankie discussed this was shocking, but Hazel mustered her mental faculties. "And you have advice?"

"You can take it or leave it."

"I'll have to hear it first, Frankie."

Frankie let out a bark of laughter and flicked a bit of ash downwind. "Alright. If you like this woman, make her *your* woman." She said this so flatly that for a moment Hazel considered it was just that easy.

"I don't think it's quite that simple."

"And why not?" Frankie looked her over and seemed to guess what she was thinking. "Because of those old men in there?" She jerked a knobby thumb over her shoulder. "They wouldn't bat an eye. They never did with me."

A small ember of hope glimmered in Hazel's chest. "And what about Raine? Shouldn't you be advocating for your niece?"

Frankie's wrinkled face twisted up in a smile. "I'm advocating for truth. You're not meant for Raine, that's plain to me. She'll find her someone. Someone she can't put on a pedestal."

"I never asked—"

"I ain't blaming you for nothing. Christ, you young'uns are so *sensitive*."

Hazel snorted quietly. "So, go marry Andy? That's your advice."

"Yeah. You know what you want. Go get it. The people that matter will be fine, and anyone who isn't, well…fuck 'em." Frankie smiled and patted Hazel's face roughly with a weathered and calloused hand. Then Frankie turned and headed back inside.

❖

Andy escorted Greg Babcock to his truck. The cracked sidewalk radiated heat. It was a sharp contrast to the coolness of her office. A clanking yellow truck creaked by and prevented them from speaking momentarily. Andy smiled and extended her hand to the ruddy-cheeked man.

"It was nice to speak with you, Mr. Babcock."

"Likewise, Ms. Richter. I'll hear from you soon?"

"Soon." She shook his hand and watched him climb into the monstrosity of a work truck. The exhaust belched and filled the air with the smell of diesel when he turned the engine over.

Andy happily returned to the cool interior of her office. She impatiently wiped away the minor sweat accumulated on her upper lip and closed her inner office door behind her. She came around her desk and scrutinized the map Greg Babcock had provided.

She traced the outline of the Parson Estate and the familiar creek that ran behind the property. It was a sprawling estate. More than one hundred acres. Bigger than the Hardy Estate she had handled previously. And all potentially purchased by one client. No hassle with an auction or cutting the farmland into tracts, and a fat bonus for her right off the top if she brokered the deal.

Andy sat heavily in her desk chair and steepled her fingers before her mouth. The bright red blaze of the cardinal flowers flashed before her eyes, as did the smooth slip of the turtle and the green coolness of the foliage as she and Hazel paddled curve after curve of that creek.

Suddenly making up her mind, Andy picked up her phone and dialed a number. After a couple of rings, Paddy's voice came over the line.

"Hello?"

"Paddy, this is Andy Richter. I have a favor to ask you."

"Ask away, my friend." He responded with a chipper tone.

"I need to get in touch with someone and I'm not sure how to go about it."

"Well, let's just see what I can do."

❖

Hazel was on her way from the hardware store back to the Corner Stop and Shop when she saw Andy standing on the sidewalk outside her office and right beside the large Babcock Construction truck. Andy smiled and shook hands with the man in the rearview.

Hazel was curious about what business a big-time construction company would have with Andy. Was Andy using them to renovate Darcy's home? She could simply ask Andy, but that brought to mind their last encounter. Hazel didn't know if she could be around Andy and not want to jump her bones. One thing was certain; she wouldn't be wearing any more tatty underpants so long as she and Andy were involved. She seemed to enjoy that black lace so *very* much. Hazel smiled at the memory.

Hazel arrived, backed the truck in by the dumpster, and started to unload her supplies. On her way back out to grab her tool bag, the large construction truck appeared at the store again. This time it parked. A man exited and looked around, spotting her with her tool bag over her shoulder.

"Your husband making you do all the work?" He laughed and held the door for her.

Hazel slipped inside and looked at Rich behind the counter. "He's not my husband."

"Good," the man replied with a conspiratorial grin at Rich. "No man worth his salt would let his wife do the heavy lifting."

Hazel ground her teeth but managed a nod and headed to the back and her project. Instead of setting straight to work, however, Hazel put down her bag and moved to the door to listen to the conversation.

"If that was my cleaning lady, I'd never get anything done," the man called loudly from the cooler where he was perusing the sodas.

"She's my boss, not my cleaning lady," Rich said stiffly.

The man laughed. "Easy there, young feller. You an' me gotta be friends. This is the only clean gas station in this town. And I'm going to be here a lot if this contract for the subdivision gets off the ground." He grasped a soda, snagged a large bag of beef jerky, and returned to the counter.

Hazel's blood ran cold. *A subdivision?* That explained the heavy-duty truck.

She waited until the man paid his tab and left before venturing from the utility closet. Rich was watching him get into his truck.

"Asshole," he muttered.

"Yeah, that's what I thought too. What was he saying about a subdivision?"

Rich turned back to Hazel and shrugged. "Just something about trying to get a contract off the ground."

"Yeah, I was afraid of that."

Rich furrowed his brow. "Wouldn't that be a good thing? Make the town bigger. Might even get an Arby's."

Hazel smiled. "Arby's would be nice, but a subdivision takes up a lot of space and means more noise, more garbage, and more traffic. All that deer and turkey hunting you do all over the county would come to an end. A subdivision would clear those pastures and woods, and that would be the end of you slipping off to your tree stand before work."

"Hadn't thought of it that way." Rich scratched his scruffy chin. "Can you stop it?"

"Me?" Hazel laughed. "What makes you think I can do anything about it?"

Rich grinned. "'Cause you're a problem solver, Hazel. I bet you could stop it if you wanted to."

The young man's faith in her was touching and put her at a loss for words. She just gave him a wink and went back to the utility closet to solve the pipe problem. This, at least, she knew how to handle.

Hazel was trying desperately to not jump to conclusions. Was Andy working with this man? The handshake and smile she'd glimpsed on her quick drive-by had not seemed particularly chummy, but maybe she was just refusing to see what was in front of her eyes. Of course Andy would want in on that sort of transaction. There was bound to be a lot of money tied up in a subdivision.

Hazel couldn't decide if she wanted to know whether Andy was involved. The idea that Andy would be willing to pave over the rural areas Hazel loved was awful. Then again, expecting Andy to understand that was, perhaps, unfair. She had not been raised in Green Valley and would not see this as a breach of faith. But the rest of the community would.

Can you stop it? Rich had asked her.

Hazel knew she would try.

❖

Andy dialed the number Paddy had provided, and the phone rang several times before a raspy voice came on the line.

"Hello?"

"Hello, Mrs. Parson?"

"This is she." There was a beat of silence. "Who is this?"

"This is Andy Richter at Richter Realty."

"Richter Realty? The only Richter I know is dead."

Andy smiled at the blunt phrase. *Straight to the point it is, then.* "That was my great-aunt Darcy," she confirmed. "I'm calling to discuss the Parson Estate. I've got an opportunity I think you would like to hear about. Can we set up a time to meet?"

Hazel looked up when her front door opened, and Paddy and Anubis walked in. She was just pulling cornbread from the oven. "Peas and cornbread alright tonight?"

"Of course." He smiled and began setting the table.

Hazel served dinner and sat down across the round table from her father. She hadn't slept well since she'd learned about Andy's possible deal with Babcock a couple of days ago. She still burned with desire for Andy, but now her feelings were tainted by her doubts.

"Enjoy." Her father would notice her tired smile, but there was nothing she could do about it.

"You feelin' alright?" He took a few bites of peas and then reached for a piece of cornbread.

"Just haven't slept well lately." She dug around in the canned jar of pepper sauce for the green tomatoes. They were her favorite.

"That pipe repair worse than you thought?"

"No, that was pretty straightforward." She regarded him thoughtfully. "Have you heard anything about a construction company driving around town? Babcock?"

He looked up with a frown. "Amos mentioned seeing a big truck. He said Frankie seemed to think it had something to do with a subdivision, but"—he waved his fork dismissively— "you know Frankie. Always thinking the worst."

"Yeah," Hazel said softly.

"Heard from Andy lately?"

Hazel shook her head. "I think we've both been pretty busy," she said evasively.

"Okay, just thought…" He trailed off for a moment. "I just thought you two were getting pretty close."

She shrugged and tried to hide the disappointment this comment brought to the surface. "Like I said, we're just busy."

"Yeah, she called here a couple of days ago wanting my help."

"Help with what?"

"Was looking for a phone number. Old Mrs. Parson."

"Parson? That's a big estate."

"That's what I thought, too." Paddy nodded and took another bite of his black-eyed peas.

Hazel sat back in her chair, putting her fork down on her plate and lapsing into silence. So, this was the property Babcock was after. The Parson Estate was a sprawling collection of pastures, fields, and woodlands…and Percy Creek. It had to be near one hundred acres, if not more. It was the perfect place for a subdivision.

"Not hungry?" Paddy's voice broke through her miserable ruminations.

"What?" He pointed at her half-finished plate. "Oh, no. I'm not hungry."

"What's really on your mind, Hazel?" Her father put down his fork, too, and stared straight at her.

She sighed. It was useless to try to keep anything from Paddy. "I know for a fact that Babcock is out here trying to set up a contract for a subdivision. I also know that Andy met with this company earlier in the week. If she's calling Mrs. Parson, it looks like she's trying to secure that property for Babcock."

Paddy sat back in his chair and wiped his mouth with a napkin before answering. "There could be another explanation."

Hazel smiled sadly at her father's optimism. "Maybe."

"Why don't you just go ask her?"

"It's complicated."

"Hmm." Paddy hummed. "I think I would rather *know*, if I were in your place, but that's your business, Wildflower."

They passed the rest of the meal without speaking. When Paddy and Anubis left after the latter cleaned the plates and the former loaded the dishwasher, Hazel sat down on her sofa and picked at a loose thread on the seam of her cotton overalls. Her fingers fumbled with the string absently as she contemplated what her father had said.

Deciding it was just best to get it over with and to stop waffling, Hazel dialed Andy's cell. She brought the phone to her ear, half-hoping Andy wouldn't answer.

"This is Andy."

Hazel's stomach wobbled at the sound of Andy's voice. "It's Hazel."

"Oh, hey."

The way Andy's voice seemed to soften at the mention of her name struck Hazel right in the chest. Her doubts twisted and tumbled in her belly like live snakes.

"I was wondering if I could come over for a minute?"

"Sure, I've got something I'd like to discuss with you anyway."

"Okay, I'll be over in about an hour."

"See you then."

CHAPTER ELEVEN

Hazel didn't know why she bothered to shower. She grumbled about the heat as she crossed the road to Andy's driveway. A cold shower had seemed like the right thing to reset her nerves and clear her head. Now, as she was once again sweating through her jean shorts and tank, Hazel cursed the heavy weight of her dark hair. She'd piled it all together and used a clip to hold it back, but just the weight of it on her scalp caused her to sweat. She reached Andy's porch with flushed skin and a less than friendly attitude.

Her demeanor was not improved by how cool Andy appeared when she opened her door.

"Next time," Hazel began as she stepped through the door into the blissfully cool foyer, "you can come visit me. I'm not making that walk again until September."

Andy grinned and drew her in for a suave kiss. She nipped at Hazel's bottom lip in a playful way and tugged at the clip in her hair. "I like you like this."

Hazel caught the cascade of dark waves and held them back with a frown. "Eww, no!"

Andy laughed and nuzzled her throat to lick the salt from her skin. "Mmm, I wonder how salty your—"

"Didn't you have something you wanted to discuss?" Hazel's pulse was through the roof. It wasn't fair that Andy affected her so strongly. Especially because there was a possibility that Andy had made a deal to sell out Green Valley. Hazel didn't know what their relationship was, but she knew she didn't want it to end because of a land deal.

Andy chuffed in her sexy way and stepped back. "I did. Would you like something to drink?"

"I think I'm alright."

"Okay, then." Andy kissed her hand and led her into the office.

The first night Hazel had been in the office, she'd been surprised to see it so transformed. For as long as she could remember, it had been an art studio. Darcy had always raved about the light in the room. Seeing how Andy had transformed the space, however, Hazel felt that the décor did fit the space. The soft, well-used leather chair and the sturdy, if worn, coffee table were inviting. The large, ornate desk was the statement piece, but it did not dominate the room. And the touch of Darcy's artwork on the walls was just perfection.

Currently, the large desk was covered in books, loose paper, and a large map. Andy drew her near and pointed out a highlighted portion of the map. "Recognize this?"

Hazel felt sick. It was the Parson Estate.

"I do." She followed the creek with her finger. "This is the creek we kayaked."

"With the cardinal flowers," Andy said softly. "I remember."

"Are you going to acquire this property?"

"Not exactly." Andy unfurled a large, rolled page on top of the map. "I'm sure you saw that big truck around town. Babcock Construction?" She weighted the page with a tumbler, a huge piece of quartz, and a bird-shaped paperweight. "This is what they want to build there."

Hazel's stomach twisted. "It's a subdivision."

"It is," Andy confirmed.

Hazel turned to her slowly and searched her face. "You're helping them do this?"

"I am not." Andy shook her head. "As a matter of fact, I'm working on something that will protect that land from being developed by anyone, ever."

Hazel's knees wobbled. "I think I need to sit down." She was weak with relief. Andy grasped her by the elbow and led her to the leather chair behind the desk.

"You thought I would sell you out?" Andy knelt before Hazel.

"No…" Hazel began but then looked at Andy with chagrin. "Well, maybe. But I was hopeful you wouldn't." She was struck with a thought. "Andy, how much money are you walking away from?"

Andy grimaced. "Enough." She stood and propped her backside on the desk. "More than I ever could have made with that fiasco of an auction."

"And you decided not to broker the deal?" Hazel asked. "Why?"

Andy turned to look out the window and the darkening woods beyond. "I couldn't stop thinking about those flowers. And that little turtle on the bank." Andy took Hazel's hand and rubbed her knuckles gently. "I never would have thought of such things before meeting you, Hazel. You got to me."

The words surged through Hazel's system like a warm beam of sun, clearing the fog of suspicion. "Is that right?"

"Just so."

Hazel stood and put her hands on Andy's waist, enjoying

how Andy's muscles tensed as she did so. She lifted her head and Andy's mouth descended. The kiss began slowly, a teasing dance of lips and tongue and sighing. Hazel was left breathless.

"Take me to bed."

❖

"Yes." Andy gasped slightly before taking Hazel's hand and leading her upstairs into the wood-paneled hallway. She brought Hazel into the last bedroom on the right and turned her around so she could kiss her again. Hazel's mouth was addictive.

Hazel pushed her back. "I want you naked this time."

"You had me nearly naked last time," Andy returned with a smile, but started to unbutton her shirt.

"*Nearly* isn't good enough. I also want you under me."

"Oh? Been thinking about this?"

"Only every day." Hazel removed her underwear and slid into bed.

Andy also slid into bed and wasted no time pulling Hazel hard to her chest and covering her mouth once again. Hazel wiggled back and then rolled Andy over. Her warm, slick center settled on Andy's stomach, and they both groaned.

"I want…"

"Tell me," Andy whispered as she slid down and wrapped her arms around Hazel's delicious thighs. She gently nipped the sensitive skin of Hazel's inner legs.

"Oh, that. That's what I want."

"This?" Andy licked the length of her, enjoying the warm, smooth feel of Hazel in her mouth.

"Yes, yes!" Hazel panted and arched above her, her heavy breasts thrust forward.

Andy dove in. Hazel flinched and ground into her mouth.

Andy wanted to take it slow. She wanted to savor every sound and tremble of Hazel's body. She wanted to drive her to the edge and hold her there indefinitely. But Hazel's need affected her. Andy had never so acutely understood the desires of a lover.

Her slow, teasing ministrations quickly became energetic as she followed the pace of Hazel's undulating hips. She reached above and molded the soft flesh of Hazel's breast in one of her hands. She pinched her nipple, eliciting a gasp from Hazel.

"Mmm…" A groan escaped Andy's throat.

Hazel covered Andy's caressing hand with her own and squeezed. "Harder," she whispered.

Andy did as she was told. She couldn't do anything else.

Hazel had been making quiet mewling noises but suddenly stiffened and cried out in release. She ground into Andy's mouth for a few seconds more before slumping forward and rolling to the side. Andy wiped her mouth on the back of her forearm and then followed Hazel to hover over her.

"Wow!" Hazel panted and cupped Andy's face. Her hand was shaking. She traced Andy's mouth reverently. "Just wow."

"You're welcome." Andy laughed. She kissed her before moving lower and finding her breasts.

Hazel grabbed her hands. "It's your turn. Let me please you."

"It would please me to touch you." Andy pressed Hazel's breasts together and nuzzled the ample cleavage.

"If you insist." Hazel ran her hands through Andy's hair, massaging her scalp and caressing the back of her neck. Andy hummed in pleasure at the sensation.

Andy alternately squeezed and released Hazel's flesh as she nipped and flicked her tongue over Hazel's left nipple. She rolled the other between her thumb and forefinger until

Hazel was panting again and rocking her pelvis up. Andy was pleased. She wanted Hazel ready to come again when she took her own pleasure.

Andy lifted her body so Hazel could not use the contact with her abdomen to stimulate herself too quickly. Hazel's eyes, which had been closed, now cracked open and looked askance at her. Andy held Hazel's gaze and bit her nipple lightly. Hazel arched her back and hissed through her teeth.

Andy straddled one of Hazel's legs and grasped the other behind the knee to raise it up. She propped Hazel's calf on her shoulder and slid their flesh together. Hazel groaned and jerked.

Andy thrust slowly and purposefully into Hazel's folds. She clenched her teeth against a growl in her throat. She had to be careful not to come undone too quickly. It would be only too easy. She nipped at the calf against her collarbone to preoccupy herself.

Hazel moved with her, picking up on the slow rhythm at once, grasping Andy's hips and trying to urge her to move more quickly. Andy chuckled, but continued her slow, steady pumping. She would not be hurried or lose herself to urgency this time.

"Andy, please..."

"When I'm ready." She pinched Hazel's nipple. "Do you think you can come again?"

"I want to."

"Mmm, good girl." Andy thrust just a bit more quickly and rotated her hips in a circular motion to cover all Hazel's exposed, sensitive flesh.

Andy admired the way the new movement jostled Hazel's breasts and caused her to arch and clench the sheets in her fists as though holding on to her last shred of sanity. The flush on Hazel's face and her shallow breathing said she was close. Andy leaned forward for better leverage and then pumped powerfully into Hazel.

The climax was instantaneous. Hazel cried out and shook with every wave of her release, but Andy didn't stop. Hazel's cry was a jolt to her system. She panted and thrust with a punishing tempo until she also crested the rise with a soft growl and began to fall.

❖

Later, Andy lay on her back with Hazel nestled in the crook of her arm, gently stroking her sternum. Hazel was so incredibly blissed out, but she was also curious about Andy's scheme.

"So, tell me about this grand plan to protect that property."

Andy seemed to come back to herself from a faraway place. "It's called a conservation easement. The gist of it is that the land is donated to a land trust. The terms of the agreement vary depending on the land, but what I'm hoping to do is establish a contract where that property can't be developed because of its conservation value."

"But why not broker a *sale* to the land trust? That way Mrs. Parson gets something out of it."

"Well, the easement doesn't necessarily mean that the property changes hands. Mrs. Parson will get to keep the estate to pass along when the time comes. She just won't be able to make any big changes like building a barn or another home or anything. It also helps decrease the property taxes on the place, so it won't be so expensive to own."

"Seems like a pretty good deal. Especially since Mrs. Parson doesn't have any kids."

"Right. Could end up with another Aunt Darcy and Andy situation."

Andy's tone was teasing, but Hazel wanted to be clear. She propped up on one arm to look Andy in the face. "That's not what I meant."

"I was kidding."

"I'm glad you came to town."

Andy cocked her head at an angle and raised a brow over her blue, blue eyes. "You are?"

"Of course I am."

"Even though I've complicated things for you?"

Hazel didn't want to talk about complications. Especially because she had not made up her mind about how to handle them. "On second thought..." She jokingly let the comment hang in the air.

Andy smiled and looked out of the window. She then checked her wristwatch. "It's half past eight." She rose from the bed and stretched before grabbing a navy silk robe. "Would you like to see what I've been working on?"

Hazel put her shorts and tank back on. She was headed home after this and would not be staying the night. She wasn't ready for that sort of commitment. She followed Andy's graceful figure down the steps and back to the study.

"How hard is it to get a conservation easement?"

"It depends on the contract. I've already called Mrs. Parson, and she's open to the idea. I have an appointment with her this weekend to formally pitch the proposition. But..." Andy looked from the documents on the desk to Hazel.

"But what?"

"I know that Babcock is going to fight me over it."

Hazel's stomach plummeted. She hadn't thought about that. "Can he do that?"

"Babcock doesn't own the property, but there is something

in the way that he talks that makes me think he's got some sort of in. It's probably a family member who stands to inherit Mrs. Parson's estate."

"Barney," Hazel said suddenly. "Barney was at the fishing tournament."

"Barney? Is he a relation?"

"Barney is Mrs. Parson's younger sister's son..." Hazel frowned as she tried to remember. "I think. Dad would know."

"And he would be the likely recipient of the Parson Estate?"

"Again, I'm not certain. Haven't seen the man in years, but he popped up a few weeks ago. Lives in Huntsville or something and is never here. Maybe it's just a coincidence."

"Maybe." Andy paused. "Babcock is out of Huntsville. Another coincidence?"

Hazel ground her teeth. "Probably not. So, Babcock couldn't fight it, but Barney could?"

"If he's set to inherit the property, he could argue that the easement would affect him negatively. I'm pretty sure I can convince the land trust otherwise, but I'd rather have a document justifying the need for conservation."

"I understand. I'm glad you thought of that. I ran into Babcock at the Stop and Shop. He struck me as a complete douchebag." Hazel had expected Andy to laugh or grin, but she did neither.

"What did he say to you?"

Andy's tone caught her by surprise. "Nothing overtly offensive, just that I was distracting."

"Did he make you uncomfortable?"

"No, babe, nothing like that. I mean, it was cringy, but I didn't feel threatened or anything." *Damn, did I just say* babe? *I'm in deep. That's alarming.*

It alarmed Hazel even more that she didn't want out.

"Okay." Andy took a deep breath and smiled in a way that didn't meet her eyes. "I know you are a smart, tough, capable woman. I didn't mean anything condescending."

"I know that." Hazel smiled. *She really does have a big heart.* "I didn't take any offense."

"Good." Andy's voice returned to a businesslike tone. "Now, do you have any ideas about conservation? I know the cardinal flowers are relatively rare, but do you know of anything else in this area that could be classified as endangered?"

"Hmm." Hazel racked her brain. "Nothing just off the top of my head. I've got a couple friends in the biology field I can contact."

"You do?"

"Sure. I majored in business, but my love was always biology. I've got a pal, Max. I'll give her a call. She might have some ideas or resources."

CHAPTER TWELVE

Hazel had decided to accompany Andy to speak with Mrs. Parson. She had helped translate what it was Andy was suggesting with the land. Mrs. Parson, for her age and lack of education, was a sharp woman. She'd asked very specific questions and had advised Andy on exactly how she expected to benefit from the easement. Even now, the memory brought a wry smile to Andy's lips.

A mosquito dive-bombed her face and brought her back to the present. She'd essentially bathed in insect repellant. As it was, the little vector was drunkenly whining back and forth, looking for a piece of unprotected skin. Andy swatted at the nuisance and her sandals slid a fraction in the silt of Percy Creek. Andy didn't know exactly why she was here. Hazel had told her to be ready to get to the creek this afternoon, and Andy had trusted Hazel's process. Andy turned her attention to Hazel.

"Your friend, Max. Was she able to offer any insight?"

"Yes, actually." Hazel led them along the shallows of the creek splashing noisily to alert the wildlife. "She mentioned an endangered crayfish that would go a long way to validating the conservation easement."

"A crayfish?"

"Yeah, you know, small crustaceans with lots of names. Crawfish, crawdads, mudbugs—"

"Mudbugs? You made that up."

"I did not!" Hazel laughed. "At any rate, Max said this one is called the slenderclaw crayfish. The best thing to do to get a glimpse is to look for a crayfish habitat and settle in for a wait."

"A *wait*?" Andy repeated as she looked around. "Just here in the creek?"

Hazel shot her a withering glance. "Would you rather climb a tree?" She gestured to the green canopy above them.

"Definitely not," Andy confirmed. "So, a crayfish habitat? What would that happen to look like?"

"Like that." Hazel pointed to an area in the stream with a large log half in the water. Around the log were several big rocks. "These critters apparently don't dig into the bank like other crayfish in the area, they hang around under stuff in the middle of the water. And they're more active later in the day, so it shouldn't be long."

Andy followed Hazel to a closer position and they both hid as best they could in the undergrowth while keeping sight of the log in the water. Andy didn't particularly like having her ass on the creekbank and her back to a wall of green. Anything could be behind her. She fought off the sensation of being watched and tried to focus on the creek.

"What do these things look like?"

"Tiny lobsters. Some of them, according to Max, are an olive-green color and some of them are mottled brown and cream. Their front claw is relatively long and slender. Hence the name slenderclaw."

"I don't plan on getting close enough to them to inspect their claws."

"Not an animal lover?" Hazel grinned at her.

"Not a big fan of crustaceans. Those legs and those claws..." Andy shuddered a bit in repulsion. "Not my thing, unless they're covered in butter."

"Fair enough."

A comfortable silence lapsed between them. Andy was continuously scanning the waterline by the log and rocks for any sign of movement. The woods around them seemed to exhale as though grateful they had stopped speaking. The sound of the forest intensified. Andy could hear birds calling to one another in the trees and something rustled softly in a thicket nearby.

She had not ventured into the wooded acres behind her late aunt's house as of yet. Hazel had assured her there was a trail to the spring and to the edge of the pasture where Hazel foraged. Andy just hadn't gotten around to exploring the land. Looking around now, perhaps she had been missing out on a worthwhile experience.

Hazel shifted beside her, her body seeming to tense. Andy's gaze slid back to the creek, and she noticed something in the water. At first, she'd taken it for a bit of debris on the surface, but the way it moved was very deliberate. Like a tiny lobster. Andy inhaled sharply. Hazel motioned for her to stay still.

The critter climbed up on the log and slowly scuttled along, stopping here and there to twitch its antennae. Hazel was doing her best to zoom in with the camera and get a good view of the small, mottled crustacean. The quiet clicking of the camera seemed impossibly loud to Andy, and she flinched every time it shuttered.

The creature suddenly dove into the water with a splash and was gone. Hazel turned to Andy; triumph was clear on her face.

"Did you get it?" Andy queried excitedly.

"I did!" Hazel perused the photos on the digital camera.

"Was that it? Was that the slenderclaw?"

"I think so! I got several really good pictures. I can sort through them when I get back to civilization." Hazel swatted at a mosquito as she spoke. "I should have quality pictures by Monday."

"Excellent." Andy smiled. *This is going to work.* "I'll file the paperwork then, too. I've got another client looking at some property in town. Maybe we could meet Tuesday at the office?"

"Sounds great."

❖

Hazel parked on the square early the next week and exited her vehicle. She could barely contain her excitement. The images she'd taken of the slenderclaw crayfish were excellent. They were crystal clear and varied in pose. She got several of the crustacean's little profile and a few of it turned and facing the camera. Hazel was supremely proud of the way the pictures had turned out and grateful they'd not had to make multiple trips to get what was needed.

The heat of the day, even at eight in the morning, was unbearable. The smell of hot asphalt and pine tar wafted to her as a logging truck trundled by. Hazel stepped onto the sidewalk from the parking spot and reached for the door of Richter Realty after a few steps. The interior of the office was cool and there was the scent of lemon. She supposed Andy had polished the oak coffee table recently. Hazel grinned at the image of Andy bent and fastidiously buffing the smooth surface of the table.

Andy poked her head around the corner of the office doorway and smiled at Hazel. "There you are. Do you have the pictures?"

"I do." Hazel crossed the space between them, brandishing the envelope of photos. "They turned out well."

Andy took them and flipped through with a serious expression. When she finished, she looked at Hazel with her cool blue eyes. "These are *great*. Exactly what we need. I've already filed the paperwork on behalf of Mrs. Parson." Andy paused to retrieve one particular photo. "This one is spectacular. It's even looking at the camera."

"They're sorta cute."

Andy wrinkled her thin nose. "I don't think I'd go that far, but I do have more appreciation for them than before. Makes me want a good lobster bisque, if I'm being honest."

Hazel laughed just as the door opened, and a tall figure filled the frame.

"You've cost me a lot of money, Richter." Greg Babcock stepped inside the office. His eyes were for Andy, but he spared Hazel a quick glance and seemed to recognize her. "Oh, in this together, are you?"

Andy stepped smoothly in front of Hazel and met the angry man head on. "I understand your frustration, Mr. Babcock—"

"I'll fight this conservation easement!" He reddened and pointed a finger in her face. "You can't stop progress."

Hazel was amazed at how cool Andy was. She stood tall with square shoulders and looked at him with a level gaze.

"You must do as you see fit, sir."

Babcock stood in the middle of the room, huffing and looking between them. He seemed ready to fight, but Andy maintained a calm air. He glanced again at Hazel, who had not moved but was watching him closely.

"And I don't know what you"—he jabbed his finger at Hazel—"have to do with all of this. But if I find out it was illegal, I'll sue you."

Hazel tried to channel some of Andy's calm. "That's your prerogative." She raised her chin an inch and glared at him.

He looked back and forth between them, his hands balled into fists. Without any other coherent comments, he turned to storm through the door. Hazel took a deep breath as Andy took her shaking hand.

"Are you okay?"

"Me?" Hazel laughed. Some of the adrenaline ebbed away as she gently cupped Andy's face. "I thought for sure he was going to hit you."

Andy shrugged. "I know a good lawyer."

Hazel laughed again, amazed by the woman before her. She was going to suggest they meet tonight, but the door opened again, and another tall figure entered.

Raine stopped dead at the door and took in the scene before her. Hazel dropped her hand from Andy's face and turned resolute eyes to Raine.

"That's the guy that wants to turn the Parson place into subdivisions." Raine gestured over her shoulder with a thumb. "And you two are working with him?"

Hazel stepped away from Andy. "Raine—"

"I could expect that from you." Raine glared at Andy who stood as calm as before. "But Hazel, I can't believe you would be in on something like this." She turned to leave.

Hazel looked at Andy, who put her hands in her pockets and raised her brows. Hazel hurried after Raine, who was already out of the door and onto the sidewalk.

"Raine! Hold up a damn minute!"

Raine stopped and whirled quickly just as Andy strode out

of the office behind Hazel. Raine glared at Andy over Hazel's shoulder. "This is your doing! We were fine until you showed up with your Italian loafers and your Mercedes. Hazel was my..." She paused and clenched her jaw. "Hazel was *my* friend before you moved here and started strutting around town."

"I don't see what my shoes or my car have to do with it," Andy replied with a smirk.

Hazel cut her eyes at Andy. "Not helpful."

"And now you're *with* her." Raine turned back to Hazel. "I thought you and I couldn't date because you wouldn't date anyone in Green Valley."

"We're not..." Hazel looked from Raine to Andy. Andy was suddenly very interested in the hood ornament on the truck next to them. Hazel took a deep breath.

"I said that to spare your feelings, Raine. I didn't want to date you, but I didn't want to reject you." The truth rang between them. Hazel knew Raine was stung. The color drained from Raine's face.

She was quiet for several moments. "Don't date me, that's fine...but *her*, Hazel?"

"What is it that I've done that offends you so?" Andy addressed Raine with a cold stare.

"You sold us out!" Raine growled.

"I did not." Andy didn't raise her voice, but it rang out nonetheless. "I have, with Hazel's help, filed paperwork to preserve that estate so that no one can build there."

Silence filled the space again. A chattering couple came down the sidewalk. The three women stepped back to allow them to pass before looking at one another again.

"Paperwork?"

"A conservation easement."

"What's that?"

"Google it," Andy snapped.

Hazel admonished Andy with a look but couldn't really blame her.

"It's just what Andy said. If it's approved, it will preserve that land and make it impossible for Babcock or anyone else to develop it."

Raine squinted at Hazel and then at Andy. She seemed to deflate a bit. After an effort Hazel admired, she squared her shoulders and looked Andy dead in the eye. "I'm sorry I misjudged you."

"I accept your apology." Andy stepped closer. "And Hazel and I are not dating, but we are exclusively involved."

Raine nodded. "I understand." She then surprised Hazel by cracking a grin. "Attagirl, Hazel."

Hazel laughed and gave her a shove. "Shut up, asshole. Now go tell your aunt she's got nothing to worry about them developing that land next to her."

"Yeah, I'll drive out there. Frankie's been shitting bricks." With a wave, Raine turned from them and climbed into her truck.

Hazel was sweating. This whole debacle had taken much more time than she had allotted for her stopover with Andy that morning. "I really need to get going, but I want to see you later."

"Tonight?" Andy asked quietly.

Hazel longed to reach out to her, to reassure them both they were okay after so much confrontation in the last half hour. She looked around for people and then drew closer and took Andy's hand.

"I'll bring dinner."

"I'm looking forward to it."

❖

Andy collapsed into her office chair and steepled her hands in front of her. She'd sweated through her cotton button-up shirt, and the collar was sticking to the back of her neck. With a grimace, she plucked at the shirt and leaned forward onto her desk.

What a morning. First, Babcock confronting her. She'd half expected that. He hadn't struck her as the sort of man to let something like that lie. Andy regretted Hazel had been there for it. Andy didn't think of her lover as delicate or fragile, but she was not rattled by such behavior. Hazel had been shaking after the encounter; her hand had trembled when Andy had taken it in her grasp. She'd barely had time to reassure them both when Raine had walked in. Once she and Hazel became involved, a confrontation had seemed unavoidable. Andy cared little for what Raine Lewis thought of her, but Raine was one of Hazel's oldest friends. Andy had tried to prepare herself for the inevitable clash.

The outcome of that skirmish had been better than she had expected. She'd misjudged Raine. A smile curved on her lips. *There's plenty of that going around.* Andy didn't expect to ever be bosom buddies with Raine, but after Raine's apology, she could certainly be friendly.

It wasn't really Raine who concerned her at the moment. It was Hazel. More specifically, it was the way Hazel had reacted to Raine's accusation that she was dating Andy. The way Hazel had wavered was right on par with the other conflicts that morning. Andy couldn't expect anything different, but it disappointed her nonetheless. As consistently as she'd striven to not have expectations, it had happened anyway.

It was impossible to not want a future with Hazel.

One domestic scene after another looped through her head like a reel of film. It was only too easy. Hazel challenged her and surprised her. She warmed her with her enthusiasm and practical encouragement. And the sex was *so* good. Andy was momentarily side-tracked as she wondered what underwear she would find under Hazel's prairie skirt tonight.

With a sigh and some effort, she pulled herself back to the present. She could only stay the course. Andy would not go back on her word and attempt to shift Hazel's boundaries. She'd told Hazel no expectations and she must abide, however excruciating it was now. Andy still had hope that Hazel would change her mind. She had to.

CHAPTER THIRTEEN

Hazel loaded dinner and a photo album into her car and set off on the brief drive across the road to Andy's house. She'd made the lasagna the night before but brought some leftover sauce to heat up and pour over to dress the dish up. She took pride in her presentation. The smell of fresh basil filled the car interior and buoyed her with a sense of everything being just right.

The day had been incredibly taxing, and she was looking forward to a nice meal and Andy's company. She owed Andy some sort of explanation for the way she had fumbled Raine's inquiry. In Hazel's defense, she wasn't into labels. Even if she were into labels, she wouldn't know what label she would assign to her and Andy's relationship.

She put this musing aside as she pulled in behind the sleek, gray coupe. Andy met her at the door with a smile. When she realized Hazel had more to unload, she stepped outside to help. Hazel pushed the photo album into her hands with a wink. Andy raised a brow, but did not comment.

"What's for dinner?"

"Lasagna."

"Mmm...I've got a nice Chianti that I think will do."

"Where did you get a *nice Chianti* around here? Or did you move in with your wine collection?"

Andy laughed. "Actually, Darcy provided the wine."

"What?"

"In addition to canned goods, Aunt Darcy kept a very expensive selection of wine in her cellar."

"Oh! Of course she did. I remember seeing her with wine. I forgot all about that. She was a woman of varied tastes."

"Indeed."

Hazel heard the wistful note in Andy's voice. That's why she'd brought the photo album.

"I brought some pictures."

"Pictures?"

"Yes. Of Darcy." Hazel set her ingredients and Tupperware on the kitchen counter. "I thought we could look at them after dinner."

"I've already got plans for after dinner."

Andy looked at her like she was a delicacy to be savored. Warmth rushed through Hazel's body. "There's no reason we can't do both."

"Good point." Andy shifted her attention to the sundry ingredients on the counter. "Now, is there anything I can help with?"

"Not really." Hazel went to the cupboards and withdrew a saucepan. "I see that a few items survived the purge." She waved the pan in Andy's direction.

"A few things. Pots and pans and such, and some random furniture. The bedroom suite remains where it is because it weighs a ton."

"So, it's more from convenience than sentimentality that you saved these things?" Hazel popped the lasagna in the oven to reheat and opened Tupperware to begin assembling her leftover sauce.

Andy grinned. "I don't know that you've noticed, but I'm not particularly sentimental."

Hazel laughed. "I had noticed."

"It doesn't mean I'm unfeeling."

"I know."

Hazel thought Andy's expression was tender as she watched Hazel chiffonade the basil. As the rich smell filled the kitchen, Andy retrieved a dark bottle. She brushed her hand at the small of Hazel's back as she squeezed past to reach into the utensil drawer for the corkscrew. The simple touch sent a shiver of arousal down Hazel's spine.

Andy poured the wine and placed a glass at Hazel's elbow before leaning in to rake her hair to the side. She pressed a delicate kiss to the back of Hazel's neck. Hazel shivered again and was certain Andy knew it. But Andy said nothing. Instead, Andy rounded the counter and sat on a stool. She pulled the photo album toward her and deliberately flipped through the pages.

Hazel watched from the corner of her eye. Andy didn't give much away in her face; her expressions were subtle. But Hazel could read them. Andy was enjoying the glimpse into Darcy's past. A small smile curled her lips.

Hazel had purposefully chosen an album that contained photos of Darcy as a young woman. She'd said it before, but Andy looked very much like her great-aunt. Hazel wanted her to see what she saw.

Andy looked up and caught her watching. Hazel smiled and reached for her wineglass.

"Dinner smells great."

"I'm glad you approve." Hazel took a sip of her wine. "Anything interesting in those photos?"

"Yes, actually." Andy looked directly into Hazel's eyes. "Was Darcy gay?"

Hazel froze. That was not what she'd expected. "What?"

Andy turned the album around and tapped a few faded pictures. "Does this not look like a group of lesbians palling around?"

Hazel squinted at the photo she'd seen dozens of times. It was Darcy on the beach with a few friends. Darcy looked glamorous, as always, in a high waisted, striped bathing suit and cat's-eye sunglasses. Her platinum hair was swept back, her head tossed toward the sun, and a beaming grin lit her face. Around her were four women, two of whom were wearing oversized, button-up shirts over their swimsuits. One of them had a cigarette in her mouth and an undeniably rakish grin.

The photo did seem more complex than a group of gal pals hanging at the beach. She looked at Andy again. Andy was clearly waiting for an answer.

"When you put it like that..." Hazel stirred the momentarily neglected sauce fervently.

"Several of these are like that." Andy pointed to another photo where the women were picnicking in a field. Darcy smiled at a woman whose head was in her lap. "This one especially." She presented a candid picture of Darcy perched elegantly on the arm of a sumptuous sofa in some undisclosed location. It looked to be a lounge. There was smoke in the air and a martini glass in her hand. The rakishly grinning woman from the beach photo stood behind her with a hand at the juncture of Darcy's neck and shoulder. "Am I wrong?"

Hazel shook her head. "No, they look like photos from a vintage lesbian magazine. Why have I never noticed that?" She lowered the heat to simmer the sauce and rounded the island to stand behind Andy as she flipped the pages. There was a more recent photo Hazel guessed was from the seventies. "There's Frankie, Raine's aunt."

"I might have guessed that. They look alike." Andy studied the picture. "I haven't met Frankie, have I?"

Hazel laughed, "No, or, believe me, you'd remember it. Frankie is Cliff's older sister."

"Is it possible Darcy and Frankie were a couple?" Andy pointed out a few more photos of the women standing together.

Hazel's head reeled. *Was it possible?* "Maybe," she admitted. "But Darcy never mentioned anything that would have made me think she was gay."

"Well, she was from a certain generation, right?" Andy flipped again and found photos of Darcy in front of her home. There were azaleas in riotous bloom behind her that the picture couldn't possibly do justice. "She wouldn't have just come out and said it, would she?"

"I guess not…" Hazel rounded the counter again to check on the lasagna and take a sip of her Chianti. "Darcy was always just so bold and up front about everything. It's hard to imagine her hiding anything…especially from me." It hurt to think Darcy wouldn't have shared this information with her.

"*You're* not out," Andy said slowly as if trying to be delicate. "Maybe Darcy was afraid of the same backlash?" She took a sip of her wine. "To be fair, I didn't know Darcy as an adult. Any memory I have of her is from the perspective of a child. I couldn't say what she thought or felt."

"You would have loved her and she you." Hazel smiled tenderly. "It is such a shame that you didn't know her."

"I have come to love her, somewhat. Through you and Paddy and this place." Andy gestured around. "Several weeks ago, you asked me if this house didn't still feel like Darcy's house, and I made some callous comment—"

"What I feel has nothing to do with it." Hazel paraphrased the lie in an affectation of Darcy's cool voice.

"I do *not* sound like that." Andy feigned a frown, but her mouth twitched, and her eyes shone with humor.

"You absolutely do!" Hazel laughed and Andy rose from the barstool to stalk toward her.

"If I ever do sound like that, it's only in an effort to seem in control around you."

"Around me?" Hazel was surprised. "What have I got to do with it?"

Andy stalked closer, and Hazel held out a hand defensively. Andy grabbed the hand and brought the palm to her lips. She kissed Hazel softly and then nipped at the skin between Hazel's forefinger and thumb.

"You have everything to do with it, Hazel Quinn." She brought their lips together and bit down on Hazel's bottom lip.

Hazel gasped and swift, hot arousal spiked in her blood. "Wait," she said softly and pulled back. "Dinner—"

"Dinner can wait."

That snapped Hazel out of her lustful stupor. "Dinner *cannot* wait, Andy Richter. You will sit and eat my lasagna."

Andy pulled back from where she had been attempting to kiss her neck. "Is it that important?"

"These noodles are homemade!"

Andy laughed and then covered her face with gentle kisses. "Of course they are. Dinner is definitely the priority. I'm sorry for suggesting otherwise."

Andy retreated to the stool and sat obediently as Hazel straightened herself and served the pasta.

❖

Later, after Andy had made good on her *after dinner* threats, Hazel lay on her side curled toward the large bay window of the bedroom. Andy spooned her from behind, breathing deeply in her sleep. The sky outside the window was the flint color of early morning with a low scudding of clouds barely discernible in the dark. Hazel gently extricated herself from Andy's arm, which was slung possessively over her hip.

She eased from the bed to grab the short robe Andy had set aside for her the night previously. The bay windows rose to the ceiling and had a cozy bench set into the nook. Hazel sat on the sun-faded seat and drew her feet up before tousling the weight of her hair over her shoulder and staring through the antique panes of glass.

The sun rising behind Andy's home was still below the tree line, and so the front view was currently bathed in a cool light that would evaporate with the dew. The magnolia trees that flanked the drive at the bottom of the knoll obscured a great deal. For all their dark, glossy foliage, however, Hazel could still see the familiar lines of her home and Paddy's tiny house in the side yard. From her current vantage point, everything looked slightly different. She'd never seen everything from this angle.

This view was a perfect metaphor for how her perspective had changed since she'd met Andy. She'd only ever rarely had a regret she'd never spoken to Paddy about her sexuality. When she did, Hazel had always reasoned it simply wasn't worth the trouble it could bring. She loved her relationship with her father, and she didn't want to know how he would respond.

But things had changed. Hazel glanced at the sleeping form of her lover. Andy had rolled to her back, an arm over her head and her mouth open. Hazel smiled as a tender warmth spread over her body and settled in her chest. She'd fallen in love with the woman quite against her own judgment. It had happened in spite of her certainty that it *couldn't* happen. And yet, upon reflection, Hazel wouldn't change a thing.

She turned back to the view out the window. She loved Andy and could not think of Green Valley without her. She couldn't imagine doing anything to hurt her, and Hazel knew, realistically, that that would be the result at this point. Hurt. Hurt for both of them. Again, she knew it came down to what mattered more to her. Andy wouldn't pressure her. She'd told Hazel she wouldn't, and Hazel trusted Andy's word. There was no one to make the decision but Hazel herself.

A stirring from the bed drew Hazel's attention from the window again. Andy propped against the headboard and stretched her sleekly muscled frame. Hazel smiled at the sight and was half ready to jump back into bed.

"Hey." Andy smiled and combed through her tangled hair with her fingers.

"Good morning."

"Coffee?"

"Of course."

Andy rose from the bed and reached for her robe and house shoes. She rounded the footboard and extended her hand to Hazel. Hazel grasped Andy's fingertips and smiled before standing and following Andy from the room.

Chapter Fourteen

A ndy set her phone on the desk and leaned back in her chair with a smile of satisfaction. The easement had gone through. It was official. She and Hazel had done it. She checked the time with a quick flick of her eyes to the wall clock. Hazel would likely be off work by now and would want to hear the good news. Andy picked up her phone again but then considered that she'd rather deliver the news in person. With a smile of anticipation at seeing Hazel, she stood, packed her bag, and locked the door behind her.

Andy pulled into the drive and parked beside Hazel's Subaru. She mounted the steps and knocked on the door.

"Come in!" Hazel called through the glass storm door.

Andy let herself in. She stopped at the threshold as the smell of biscuits hit her. The scent of something else, something like potatoes, hung in the air as well. God, the woman could cook.

"Hey."

"Hey!" Hazel responded with a smile as she pulled a pan of biscuits from the oven. "What are you up to?"

Andy crossed the room and leaned on the island. "Do I have to be up to something?"

"Hmm." Hazel arched a brow. "Would you like to stay for dinner?"

"What are you cooking?"

"Does it matter?"

Andy grinned in response. "No." She laughed. "It doesn't matter. I'll eat what you put in front of me."

Hazel grinned wickedly. "I know that already."

Andy's pulse responded to the innuendo, and she came around the counter to bring them closer. "Is that so?"

"Don't start anything." Hazel held a protective hand over her skillet and laughed.

"Me?" Andy grasped her hips from behind, mindful of the stove, and pressed her pelvis into Hazel's backside. "I would never."

"Andy…" Hazel's words warned her, but her voice was breathy and hitched at the end.

Andy stepped back reluctantly. As much as she wanted her hands on Hazel, she didn't want to distract her while she had a sizzling pan before her. "If you insist."

With a flick of her wrist, Hazel set the burner to simmer and turned to face Andy. She wiped her hands on a paisley towel. "Now you have my full attention. What is it you need, Andy Ritcher?" she asked in a playful tone.

"I got a call today…The conservation easement we filed has been confirmed."

Hazel clapped a hand over her mouth and beamed. "Really? And Babcock?"

"Apparently he let them know exactly what he thought of me." Andy grinned wryly.

"I'm sure you were gutted."

"Heartbroken," she confirmed in a mocking tone. "But this means that the property is safe. They can't touch it. No one can touch it."

"Oh, my God, Andy. That is amazing." Hazel drew her face down.

Andy met Hazel's mouth eagerly. Her arms automatically encircled her waist, and she pulled Hazel snugly to her chest to relish the feel of her in her arms. Before Andy truly had time to sink into the experience, however, there was a soft clicking noise and then the creak of a door.

Hazel jumped away from her as though she'd been scolded. Andy noticed the flaming blush on her face as Hazel crossed to the refrigerator as though trying to put as much distance between them as possible in the small kitchen. Andy turned to the door to see Paddy stepping across the threshold with Anubis on his heels. She looked back at Hazel, who would not meet her eyes, and a bubble burst in her chest, filling her gut with ice water.

Andy turned to Paddy with a forced smile. "Hey there, how are you?"

"Andy!" He smiled broadly. "I'm just peachy. Staying for dinner?"

"Actually, I've got a few loose ends to tie up." She would not look at Hazel and feel that sinking disappointment all over again. "I just came by to tell Hazel that the conservation easement had been confirmed."

"Well, that's wonderful news!" Paddy grabbed her hand and looked her in the eye. His amber eyes were so much like Hazel's that Andy had to stare at his forehead instead of meeting his gaze. "Are you sure you won't stay for dinner?"

The ice churned in her belly. "I'm sure." She patted his hand and then dropped it. "I just stopped by for a quick minute." Andy turned but did not lock eyes with Hazel. "Goodbye, Hazel."

Without waiting for a reply, she patted Anubis on the head and strode through the door.

❖

Hazel had fucked up. Half of her wanted to chase after Andy and the other half wanted to slink into a hole for eternity. The look on Andy's face had been pure hurt and disappointment, and as many times as she reminded herself they'd agreed on *no expectations*, she couldn't swallow the acrid taste of regret. She'd cut Andy—cut her unintentionally, but cut her deeply nonetheless.

And for what? To preserve the image of casual friendship? To keep Paddy in the dark? She glanced at her father and knew he knew something was off. Even Anubis had whined after Andy when she walked through the door. Suddenly, a burning smell wafted to her on the air, and Hazel whirled in horror. The potatoes!

"Shit!" She grabbed a pot holder and pulled the cast iron from the eye quickly, but the damage had been done. The potatoes were scalded on the bottom. "Damn!" She glared at the door where Andy had disappeared but knew it was her own fault for being so distracted.

Paddy stood quietly back, far out of the way, but with a concerned expression on his face. "Are you alright, Wildflower? You haven't burned anything in fifteen years."

Hazel turned off the burner and dropped the pan back to the stove with a loud clang. "No, I'm not alright."

"Well, why don't we just grab some potato chips and sit on the porch for a bit, then?"

Hazel tried to smile at him, but all she could muster was a grimace. "Alright, but I need to put away the biscuits—"

He waved his hand dismissively. "No, you go sit down. I can wrangle that."

"Alright, Pops." She headed for her favorite rocking chair.

When she opened the door, the thick, humid heat rolled over her. The sound of the cicadas was a steady, busy, buzz in the still air. Hazel sat and added the creaking of the rocker to the cacophony.

Paddy emerged with three different bags of potato chips and a couple of mugs of beer. "I put the biscuits in the pantry and made us a shandy." He offered her one mug and the bag of dill pickle chips.

Hazel relaxed incrementally as she took the frosted glass. "Thank you."

He sat and opened his extreme cheese potato chips, then fit her with a penetrating look over his conservative wire-rimmed glasses. "Now, just you tell me everything that's been going on, Hazel."

And she did. Staring across the road to the tree line behind Andy's house, Hazel's thoughts poured out like a river. She wanted to be spare in the details, but talking felt so good. Paddy was silent. He would nod or tilt his head from time to time, but he did not interrupt or ask questions. He simply let her talk.

"And now, I'm afraid I've hurt her terribly." Hazel tried desperately to keep the emotional tremble from her voice.

Her father sat back and took a sip of his shandy. "Why didn't you tell me before?" His voice was sad, but not accusing or judgmental.

"I was afraid," Hazel answered honestly. "Which was dumb, I guess."

"Fear isn't always rational. I just wish I could have helped in some way."

Hazel looked directly at him for the first time since she began speaking. "You're not upset or disappointed?"

"Disappointed?" He raised his eyebrows. "In something as trivial as your romantic preferences?"

Hazel blinked. "But the Bible…" She didn't know what exactly she was arguing. "Leviticus, Romans, Corinthians, the list goes on and on. There is a great deal written about sexual immorality."

"That's true," Paddy acknowledged. "But Jesus spoke more against corruption and greed than anything else. Luke 16 is particularly specific, and yet, as a culture, we still worship wealth. And Christians are some of the worst."

Hazel mulled this over. "So, what exactly are you saying?"

"I'm saying that I like Andy, and I love you. I'm not worried about your decisions or choices because I trust you." He answered simply and in a gentle tone. "If you want to make it work with Andy, you should go for it."

Hazel laughed, relieved and elated at the same time. "You sound like Frankie."

"Do I?" He smiled. "I think I told her the same thing one time."

"Really?"

"And she and Darcy did make a good try of it, but Darcy didn't want to commit."

Hazel was stunned. "Frankie and Darcy?"

"Yup." He nodded and took a sip of his shandy. "But neither could compromise."

"I won't make that mistake," Hazel said softly.

Paddy looked at her. "What are you waiting for? March on over there."

Hazel wanted to offer more than a simple apology. Struck with inspiration, she grinned. "I have a better idea."

CHAPTER FIFTEEN

Andy was running late. This was exactly what she did not need on a Monday morning. She was in a foul mood; she'd not slept well in three days because she couldn't get Hazel's rejection out of her head. It still stung her just as much as it had when it happened.

After the encounter the previous week, Andy had returned to her empty home and sat in the darkening space of her den. She was ashamed of her idiocy. She'd known to not get involved with a closeted woman. She'd convinced herself she could wait for Hazel to come around. That Hazel would eventually see things from Andy's perspective and that they would live happily ever after. She cringed at her naïveté. To top it all off, Hazel had not called nor texted her once over the weekend.

It was well and truly over.

Andy visited the Corner Stop and Shop on her way to town, like she did every Monday morning. She topped off her tank and then stepped inside to get a homemade chicken biscuit. When she got through the door, the young man behind the counter flagged her down with a grin.

Surprised and a little suspicious, Andy detoured to the register first. "Good morning."

"Mornin'!" He pushed a bag her way. "Your breakfast has been paid for today."

Andy frowned. "What?"

"Someone paid for your—"

"I heard you." She paused and forced herself to be calm. "Who paid for it?"

"It's a secret."

"A secret," she repeated, nonplussed.

"A surprise." He winked.

"Right." She took the bag and the hot coffee and took a tentative sip. The mystery person had even gotten her coffee order correct. "Well, if they come in again, thank them for me."

"Sure thing!"

His exuberance was a bit much for her, so Andy just nodded and exited the store. Once in her car, she opened the bag to find her usual breakfast order complete with a stack of napkins and mustard packets. One of the napkins had blocky writing on it. She pulled it from the bag and read the message.

Andy, I just want to say...

Andy flipped the napkin over. Nothing. She pilfered through the other napkins and scrutinized the wrapper of the biscuit. She even looked under her coffee lid. Nothing. No other writing. *What the hell is going on?*

❖

Andy finished her breakfast and by midmorning had gotten so involved in her work she'd forgotten about the mysterious message. Then Gavin walked into her office and knocked on her door.

"Ms. Ritcher, I just wanted to let you know we're about to start on your car."

Andy blinked several times. "Start on my car?"

"Yeah, with the wash, you know?"

Physically shaking her head, Andy stood from behind her desk. "What are you talking about?"

Gavin frowned. "You didn't call about a car wash?"

"A car wash?"

"Yeah, somebody called and said you wanted a car wash. Can't say I blame you. If someone did that to my car—"

Andy didn't wait for him to finish. She pushed brusquely past him and was out the door. The sudden sunlight and heat hit her like a wall, but she strode to her coupe to find that someone had chalked her windshield.

She read the message.

I'm sorry.

"What the hell is going on?" She growled. The two boys preparing to help Gavin with the graffiti faltered. She rounded on the young man behind her. "Who called you?"

He looked a bit perturbed but answered calmly. "I thought it was you." He scratched his chin. "Do you still want a wash? It's paid for."

Andy raked a hand through her hair. "I guess so. I can't drive around like that, can I?"

"No, ma'am." Gavin shook his head solemnly. "We will take care of it, won't we, guys?"

"Yes, ma'am." The two young men answered simultaneously.

Andy would have found the reaction funny if she wasn't

so perplexed and wrong-footed. "Well, alright, then." She returned to her office.

She sat down heavily in her chair and pressed the heels of her hands to her eyes. *What is going on?* She opened the top drawer of her desk and pulled out the napkin from the gas station that morning. Obviously the two messages went together. A single person was orchestrating this. But no one owed her an apology, except Babcock and Hazel.

Andy shook her head and tucked the napkin away. Babcock would definitely *not* apologize like this, and Hazel wouldn't do something so public. Especially not when Andy had not heard from her all weekend. *Andy, I just want to say I'm sorry.*

She hoped whatever needed to be said had been said.

❖

At five till twelve, Andy placed the phone back in its receiver on her desk and rolled out the tension in her neck. She'd gotten a lot accomplished. She felt especially good about a possible deal for a ranch home just outside the city limit. The potential buyer was a veterinarian looking to establish a local practice. Andy had enjoyed speaking with her.

Pushing back from her chair, she rose with a few pops and snaps in her spine. It was lunchtime and she considered calling the local deli for their club sandwich. Her mouth watered at the idea of fresh tomatoes and salty bacon.

Before she could dial their number, however, the door to her business opened again. Andy came out of her office to find a teenage girl with a paper bag in hand.

"Club with chips, extra mustard." She held out the bag.

"What?" Andy was surprised the bizarre chain of events

continued. The confusion was wearing off, but the wariness was not.

"Your order, right? Salt and vinegar chips are in the bag."

Andy took the bag, and the girl popped her gum, turned quickly, and forcefully exited the door. Andy noticed writing on the paper sack. She hurried to her desk to empty the contents of the bag and smooth the brown paper so she could read the message.

I promise...

"I promise"? I promise what?

Andy paced her office. Back and forth she went, glaring at the paper bag and her lunch. *Who else but Hazel?* As soon as the thought rose, however, Andy squashed it. She'd already been burned, she wasn't going to be caught dreaming again. Still...Andy sat, pushed the bag away and then unwrapped her sandwich. Might as well eat while she waited for the next message.

As it happened, she didn't have long to wait. Fifteen minutes after she finished her sandwich, her door opened once again. Full of suspicion, Andy strode into the outer room to find an elderly lady with a box in her hands.

"Good afternoon."

"Good afternoon," Andy replied. "Let me guess. It's already paid for."

The woman looked surprised. "Why yes, it is. I did the icing myself." She passed the box to Andy. Inside was a small, beautiful cake.

"Caramel cake?"

"That's right, honey."

The message was written in chocolate icing.

…to love and cherish you.

It had to be Hazel. No one else knew she loved caramel cake. "It's lovely. Thank you."

"Don't thank *me*," the woman said with a wink. She put her wrinkled hands together and then left.

Andy took the cake back to her office and sat down. She stared at the powder blue box. *Hazel.* A smile turned up the edges of her mouth. Warmth began in her chest and spread to her crown and to her toes. This was the apology she wanted but had been afraid would not come. Hazel had gone out of her way to involve half the town. Andy understood the bravery it took for her to do this and fell in love with Hazel all over again. She wondered if there were more messages on the way.

She considered what Hazel's apology meant for her. For them. Andy opened the box and retrieved the fork she always washed and reused. The first bite was heaven. And so was the second. She leaned back in the chair with a sigh and contemplated where they would go from here. She understood Hazel's distaste for labels, but all of this seemed to signal Hazel's willingness to adopt one. What she really needed was to sit and have a conversation with Hazel about her intentions. Andy took a few more bites of the delightfully sticky caramel cake and then put it aside. She wanted to save some for later.

It was difficult to turn her mind back to work, but she had a meeting with a client at three o'clock and needed to prepare. There were no additional interruptions to her workday. She was grateful. Andy wasn't sure how much more suspense she could take. She was ready to have resolution with Hazel, one way or another. When the client left, she packed her briefcase and drove home.

When Andy pulled past the magnolia trees at her driveway entrance, she hit the brakes. Her porch was a dynamic canvas of color. There were flowers and shrubs and trees. Dozens of varieties sitting in pots and containers. They lined the steps and the railings and some even sat out in front of the house. She was reminded of Paddy's greenhouse. Andy searched the vibrant riot for any clue of its origin, and her gaze landed on Hazel, sitting on the steps in the middle of it all. Rather than drive to her backdoor as was customary, Andy parked the car in the drive. She tried to calm the butterflies in her stomach as she slid from the coupe and walked toward the porch.

Hazel stood as Andy approached and leaned against the railing of the steps.

"I've had an unusual day," Andy said.

"Oh?" Hazel grinned. "Tell me about it."

"Well, some unnamed admirer bought my breakfast, my lunch, and a whole cake for dessert. They also chalked my car and then paid for it to be washed."

"Really? Bizarre."

"That's what I thought. What's more is that they left me a message with every action."

"Oh, like this?" Hazel descended the steps to meet her on the ground and handed her a card with the full message.

Andy, I just want to say I'm sorry. I promise to love and cherish you if you'll still have me.

She had underlined the last five words.

Andy smiled as she read the card and then looked at Hazel. "You went through an awful lot of trouble." She admired all of the flowers. "Did you call every nursery in the county?"

"I did, actually. One was closed and one was too busy today, but all the others rose to the occasion."

Andy laughed and leaned closer to inspect the plants and realized she recognized many of them. "All this for me?"

"Every bit of it." Hazel watched Andy as she scanned the flowers and foliage. "I knew that you wanted to revitalize the grounds and garden beds. All of these things are native to this area and will attract bees, birds, and butterflies. Paddy even threw in one of his treasured flame azalea shrubs. It will all be a lot of work, but it will be worth it."

"I'm not afraid of putting in work." Andy met Hazel's gaze. Happiness and comfort welled inside her. *She loves me.* "A simple apology would have worked."

Hazel shook her head and took her hand. "No, babe, it wouldn't. You're worth so much more than that, and I should have made that clear before now. I love you and I want to be with you openly. If that's what you want, of course."

The small amount of uncertainty in her voice caused Andy's heart to ache. "That's what I want. It's what I've wanted from the beginning." She took Hazel in her arms and brought their mouths together to illustrate her sincerity. When they separated, Andy motioned toward her front door. "What was Paddy's part in this?"

Hazel laughed. "How did you know?"

Andy ascended the steps behind Hazel, admiring the view. "You tell your dad everything. Now, what did he suggest? Was it the cake?"

"It was the window chalk on your car, actually."

Andy pretended to clutch her chest. "The scoundrel!"

"Oh!" Hazel whirled quickly around to look at her, excitement in her eyes. "And he confirmed your theory about Frankie and Darcy."

Andy stopped in the act of opening the front door. "You're kidding."

So, Paddy had known about Darcy all along. He had probably known about Andy and Hazel all along, too. Andy already held Paddy Quinn in high esteem, but she felt a surge of affection for him.

"Not at all." Hazel looked at Andy's stumped face with a small chuckle. "Pour me some bourbon and I'll give you a summary."

"Deal, but I want the *details*. We've got all the time in the world." Andy smiled and led Hazel into her home.

About the Author

Jo Hemmingwood lives in an enchanted wood in rural Alabama with her wife, children, and a menagerie of animals. Her first novel, *Broken Fences*, was nominated for a Goldie in the Debut Novelist Category in 2024, and her second novel, *Promises to Protect*, was published in June 2024. Jo's varied life experience is reflected in her craft, and her writing is often humorous and personal. She pulls from her Southern rural upbringing to create stories about community and shared experiences. This is her third novel.

Books Available From Bold Strokes Books

An Extraordinary Passion by Kit Meredith. An autistic podcaster must decide whether to take a chance on her polyamorous guest and indulge their shared passion, despite her history. (978-1-63679-679-6)

Heart's Appraisal by Jo Hemmingwood. Andy and Hazel can't deny their attraction, but they'll never agree on the place they call home. (978-1-63679-856-1)

That's Amore by Georgia Beers. The romantic city of Rome should inspire Lily's passion for writing, if she can look away from Marina Troiani, her witty, smart, and unassumingly beautiful Italian tour guide. (978-1-63679-841-7)

Through Sky and Stars by Tessa Croft. Can Val and Nicole's love cross space and time to change the fate of humanity? (978-1-63679-862-2)

Uncomplicate It by Kel McCord. When an office attraction threatens her career, Hollis Reed's carefully laid plans demand revision. (978-1-63679-864-6)

The Unexpected Heiress by Cassidy Crane. When a cynical opportunist meets a shy but spirited heiress, the last thing she plans is for her heart to get involved. (978-1-63679-833-2)

Vanguard by Gun Brooke. Beth Wild, Subterranean freedom fighter, is in the crosshairs when she fights for her people and risks her heart for loving the exacting Celestial dissident leader, LaSierra Delmonte. (978-1-63679-818-9)

Wild Night Rising by Barbara Ann Wright. Riding Harleys instead of horses, the Wild Hunt of myth is once again unleashed upon the world. Their ousted leader and a fey cop must join forces to rein in the ride of terror. (978-1-63679-749-6)

A Thousand Tiny Promises by Morgan Lee Miller. When estranged childhood friends Audrey and Reid reunite to fulfill their best friend's dying wish, the last thing they expect is a journey toward healing their broken friendship and discovering a newfound love for each other. (978-1-63679-630-7)

Behold My Heart by Ronica Black. Alora Anders is a highly successful artist who's losing her vision. Devastated, she hires Bodie Banks, a young struggling sculptor, as a live-in assistant. Can Alora open her mind and her heart to accept Bodie into her life? (978-1-63679-810-3)

Fearless Hearts by Radclyffe. One wounded woman, one determined to protect her—and a summertime of risk, danger, and desire. (978-1-63679-837-0)

Stranger in the Sand by Renee Roman. Grace Langley is haunted by guilt. Fagan Shaw wishes she could remember her past. Will finding each other bring the closure they're looking for in order to have a brighter future? (978-1-63679-802-8)

The Nursing Home Hoax by Shelley Thrasher and Ann Faulkner. In this fresh take for grown-ups on the classic Nancy Drew series, crime-solving duo Taylor and Marilee investigate suspicious activity at a small East Texas nursing home. (978-1-63679-806-6)

The Rise and Fall of Conner Cody by Chelsey Lynford. A successful yet lonely Hollywood starlet must decide if she can let go of old wounds and accept a chance at family, friendship, and the love of a lifetime. (978-1-63679-739-7)

A Conflict of Interest by Morgan Adams. Tensions rise when a one-night stand becomes a major conflict of interest between an up-and-coming senior associate and a dedicated cardiac surgeon. (978-1-63679-870-7)

A Magnificent Disturbance by Lee Lynch. These everyday dykes and their friends will stop at nothing to see the women's clinic thrive and, in the process, their ideals, their wounds, and a steadfast allegiance to one another make them heroes. (978-1-63679-031-2)

Big Corpse on Campus by Karis Walsh. When University Police Officer Cappy Flannery investigates what looks like a clear-cut suicide, she discovers that the case—and her feelings for librarian Jazz—are more complicated than she expected. (978-1-63679-852-3)

Charity Case by Jean Copeland. Bad girl Lindsay Chase came home to Connecticut for a fresh start, but an old, risky habit provides the chance to save the day for her new love, Ellie. (978-1-63679-593-5)

Moments to Treasure by Ali Vali. Levi Montbard and Yasmine Hassani have found a vast Templar treasure, but there is much more to the story—and what is left to be found. (978-1-63679-473-0)

The Stolen Girl by Cari Hunter. Detective Inspector Jo Shaw is determined to prove she's fit for work after an injury that almost killed her, but a new case brings her up against people who will do anything to preserve their own interests, putting Jo—and those closest to her—directly in the line of fire. (978-1-63679-822-6)

Discovering Gold by Sam Ledel. In 1920s Colorado, a single mother and a rowdy cowgirl must set aside their fears and initial reservations about one another if they want to find love in the mining town each of them calls home. (978-1-63679-786-1)

Dream a Little Dream by Melissa Brayden. Savanna can't believe it when Dr. Kyle Remington, the woman who left her feeling like a fool, shows up in Dreamer's Bay. Life is too complicated for second chances. Or is it? (978-1-63679-839-4)

Goodbye Hello by Heather K O'Malley. With so much time apart and the challenges of a long-distance relationship, Kelly and Teresa's second chance at love may end just as awkwardly as the first. (978-1-63679-790-8)

Emma by the Sea by Sarah G. Levine. A delightful modern-day romance inspired by *Emma*, one of Jane Austen's most beloved novels. (978-1-63679-879-0)

One Measure of Love by Annie McDonald. Vancouver's hit competitive cooking show *Recipe for Success* has begun filming its second season, and two talented young chefs are desperate for more than a winning dish. (978-1-63679-827-1)

The Smallest Day by J.M. Redmann. The first bullet missed—can Micky Knight stop the second bullet from finding its target? (978-1-63679-854-7)

To Please Her by Elena Abbott. A spilled coffee leads Sabrina into a world of erotic BDSM that may just land her the love of her life. (978-1-63679-849-3)

Two Weddings and a Funeral by Claudia Parr. Stella and Theo have spent the last thirteen years pretending they can be just friends, but surely "just friends" don't make out every chance they get. (978-1-63679-820-2)

Firecamp by Jaycie Morrison. Going their separate ways seemed inevitable for two people as different as Fallon and Nora, while meeting up again is strictly coincidental. (978-1-63679-753-3)

Coming Up Clutch by Anna Gram. College softball star Kelly "Razor" Mitchell hung up her cleats early, but when former crush, now coach Ashton Sharpe shows up on her doorstep seven years later, beautiful as ever, Razor hopes the longing in her gaze has nothing to do with softball. (978-1-63679-817-2)

Fixed Up by Aurora Rey. When electrician Jack Barrow and artist Ellie Lancaster get stuck on a job site during a blizzard, close quarters send all sorts of sparks flying. (978-1-63679-788-5)

Stranded by Ronica Black. Can Abigail and Whitley overcome their personal hang-ups and stubbornness to survive not only Alaska but a dangerous stalker as well? (978-1-63679-761-8)

Whisk Me Away by Georgia Beers. Regan's a gorgeous flake. Ava, a beautiful untouchable ice queen. When they meet again at a retreat for up-and-coming pastry chefs, the competition, and the ovens, heat up. (978-1-63679-796-0)

www.ingramcontent.com/pod-product-compliance
Lightning Source LLC
Chambersburg PA
CBHW030527020726
47494CB00004B/1259